Adrian

CLONE CITY

JOYPOLIS 1

Joypolis 1: Clone City
Copyright © 2017 Adrian Peters

The right of Adrian Peters to be identified as the author of this work has been asserted by him in accordance with the Copyright, Designs and Patents Act 1988.

All rights reserved. No part of this publication may be reproduced, stored in a retrieval system, or transmitted in any form or by any means, electronic, mechanical, photocopying, recording or otherwise, except by a reviewer who may quote brief passages and reproduce the cover for a review, without the prior permission of the publisher.

Cover design from an idea by Adrian Peters developed by bookwebs.co.uk

ISBN-13: 978-1545512432
ISBN-10: 1545512434

Printing history
First edition: June 2017

Contents

Prologue	1
Packer Ord	7
The Home Affairs Committee	13
Silver Lines	21
The Alzaris	29
At Home	35
The Chairman	41
Chance	49
A Meeting of Minds	57
The Outside	69
The Watchers	75
A Word	81

Any Other Business	85
Laia	91
D and Z	97
Valchek's Secret	101
Remorse	105
An Arm	111
Junked	117
The Banquet	125
Now or Never	129
Emergency	135
The March	145
Man Ord	151
The Calm	155
The Headline	161
O	167
The Storm	177

Prologue

Eyes skyward, the survivors pray: please let it be the last. Please God, make it stop.

When the last asteroid blazes across the sky, Earth's civilizations lie in ruins shrouded in silence.

Beneath ash-laden skies, people herd together and wander in search of food and fertile land. Although many revert to lawlessness and savagery, all face the same gargantuan task – to re-stake the claim of humankind to the territory of Earth.

The best chance falls to a group of scientists who emerge from a hive of underground shelters that contain state-of-the-art laboratories. At the head of several hundred, they erect a bio-dome and begin to farm the land. As the atmosphere clears, the dome is dismantled and work begins on building a tower to act as a beacon to others less fortunate than themselves. They name their settlement Joypolis in the hope that it will be the first of many to follow. But, when every wanderer who reaches their sanctuary dies of radiation sickness, Joypolitans begin to believe it would be suicidal to venture beyond the perimeter of their settlement.

After three generations, a crisis looms – the birth rate continues to fall. Trauma is blamed and the leaders propose cloning as the only way to produce the numbers required to develop a modern city. One political faction, the Andradists, vehemently oppose their plan and argue for the use of intelligent machines instead. When their alternative is rejected, they attempt to seize power by violent means. Overcome, they are driven out of the city on pain of death should they ever attempt to return.

Following their exile, the Clone Acts become law. Among the Acts' many articles, one states that all cell contributions are the property of the state and will remain anonymous. Another stipulates that contributions will be held for at least one generation before they are used. This 'first-generation rule' helps overcome objections to the indoctrination of clones by means of bio-semiotics – a science based on groundbreaking advances in how language is processed in the brain.

As predicted, when the numbers reach a critical threshold, the project ushers in an age of rapid development. In a relatively short time, Joypolis is transformed into a technologically advanced city that appears to have overcome all the challenges of its turbulent past. The battle for survival has been won and the future of humankind assured. Or is it?

***

Sovran, the Director of Media, stood gazing out of the window of her luxury apartment. Beyond the city, as far as the eye could see, was forest – a green patchwork undulating far into the distance. Pursing her lips, she wondered how much longer they could carry on ignoring the Outside. The subject had become taboo and the very word unmentionable in polite society.

Ever since the catastrophe, the remit of Media had been to keep the morale of survivors high – even if it meant hiding the truth. And it did – the truth of just how devastated the planet was. But it's different now, she thought. The Outside is renewing itself. Each year, the forest became greener and more vibrant. How much longer could they go on ignoring this? Surely it was time to venture Out? To turn the vision of the Founders into a reality by making Joypolis, not the *last*, but the first of many cities.

She sighed. The citizens would have to face their fears one day. It would mean unravelling all the illusions that Media had so carefully hung in their minds. If they didn't, and something unexpected happened, all those comforting beliefs would come crashing down. It'd be bad, far worse than a controlled conversion.

And then there were the clones, she thought, pushing her hand deep into her glossy black hair. How, she wondered, could their forbears have accepted the production of a human underclass so easily?

***

Gorvik, Director of Cloning and Socialization, read the message that popped up onto his computer screen. His request for a meeting to discuss the advantages of free cloning had been turned down again. 'Can't even discuss the bloody issue,' he growled, getting up so abruptly that his chair spun away on its wheels. Looking around, he wished there was a bag he could pound his fists into.

Pacing up and down, he fumed inwardly. The city was full of LPRs – Low Personal Responders, cloned from banked tissue and egg donations according to Clone Act regulations. These were the uncomplaining, low-paid workforce that supported the high standard of living that every citizen enjoyed. No wonder nobody wants to address the issue, he thought. Leave the status quo as it is. Why spoil a good thing?

But how much longer can we carry on like this, he asked himself for what seemed the thousandth time. It's as if we've strapped ourselves into an intellectual straitjacket. Can't talk about this, can't talk about that! We're stagnating when we most need to progress!

'Shit,' he swore as he sloshed a brandy into a glass. Swigging it down and feeling its heat burn back, he tried to calm his thoughts. Yes, he mused, it may have been all right at the beginning: the survivors were so traumatized the birth rate fell and cloning was the quickest way of getting the numbers needed to build a modern city. But we should have started cloning for intelligence and not left the project as a... slave production line. Because that's all it is – whatever platitudes Media may use. Can't go on. Initiative's being undermined. If we don't get rid of them soon, the whole system will grind to a halt. We've got to clone for intelligence!

Slowly, he put his glass down and began twiddling his red beard into a point as he pieced together a plan. If I can't get them to listen, I'll force them to by...

***

Q'zar, Director of Security, tried to ignore the razzmatazz blaring from a speaker above an entrance to the Pink Zone. 'Come, come! Climb the vine of ecstasy! She's yours, all yours, waiting to live your dream...' He quickened his pace. The cheap glitter of this district sickened him. For him, it was clear proof that Joypolis had lost its sense of purpose. He thought of Zuriko Azari, the woman who controlled the sex industry. Damn her, he swore.

Reaching his vehicle, he got in, slid the door shut and sank back in the seat. Facing him were the neon signs that crowned the cluttered buildings of the Pink Zone. He watched them digitally draw and flesh out the ample curves of their products, set their eyelashes fluttering, breasts bouncing, asses wriggling.

What, he thought, would the Founders think if they could see this? They wouldn't recognize the city they'd struggled so hard to establish. They never intended this... this, decadence. Joypolis was never meant to be the last city; it was supposed to be the first of many more. Perhaps it's time he thought, shooting a wary glance down a road that led to the city's perimeter.

Tiredly, he reached forward to push the starter button when, catching sight of some clones in his rear-view mirror, he paused. He eyed them coldly as they ambled along, laughing and joking. Growers, he thought, noting the emblem on their sleeves as they passed toward the Pink Zone.

He stared at their backs a few more seconds before pushing the starter. As the vehicle glided forward guided by roadside sensors, Q'zar began to wonder, what if we sent some clones Out? That way we needn't risk exposing ourselves to radiation or whatever other dangers there may be. We could find out why that grey area of forest keeps getting closer. Who knows, perhaps we need to strengthen our defences. Code knows, we've had so many years of peace we've become complacent. What if there is something Out there that poses a threat? If only we had a leader with vision!

***

Ignoring the drone of voices around the table, Darvin, Joypolis' most powerful politician, sat drumming his fingers on its polished surface. He'd grown tired of chairing meetings. How they dragged on. He leaned back in his chair to see if he could get a better view of the white triangular roof of the Aesthetics School. He could just make out its edges shimmering in the haze of heat.

He wondered if Zuriko, the head of the School, was dreaming of him as he was of her. How he longed to fill his nostrils with her perfumed fragrance and slide dreamily down the scented trail of her smooth barley-coloured skin to lose himself in the forgiving forgetfulness of pleasure.

Oh, Codes, he thought, coming back to reality with a jolt as someone squeakily insisted, 'No, no, no. This will never do. It has to be amended. Point three of Article 5a should read 'and' not 'or'!'

Groaning inwardly, he recalled a line from a poet of the Old World: 'pinnacled dim in the intense inane'. How apt, he thought.

***

O was a noble who had turned his back on politics to wander the streets in search of enlightenment. Sitting on a low wall in the shade of an artificial tree, he watched citizens rushing hither and thither. Like shadows chasing shadows, he thought. Looking up at the glittering windows of high-rise buildings spiking the sky, he wondered is it a house of cards and am I the fool, the jester fallen from the pack, when I ask what's happened to the wanderlust, the questing spirit of the people? Look at them! As much running from as hurrying to. Happily, satisfyingly distracted. Have they lost it? This, the city that holds the fate of humankind and they, its lifeblood, racing to the next purchase!

Change will come, he thought, getting up and dusting down his baggy trousers. But from where? he wondered as he shuffled away.

Packer Ord

It seemed like any other day at the Hub. As canned goods came bobbing along a conveyor belt, clones packed them into boxes. Further along, the boxes were sealed so that when they reached the end of the line they could be pulled off onto the floor to be sorted. Once sorted, they were stacked onto trolleys and driven off down the broad lanes that intersected the rows of shelves that criss-crossed the warehouse floor.

When a trolley arrived at the section designated for its goods, a Packer would step forward and check that they corresponded with the numbers on his docking sheet. If they did, he unloaded them. When the trolley purred off, he would begin stacking them onto the shelves before another came along.

High above the shelves and suspended from the ceiling by cables were transparent tubular walkways. They radiated out from a central hub to the administrative offices that lined the surrounding walls. It was this pattern that had given the warehouse its name – the Hub. Sometimes, managers would pause while crossing to view the work of clones below. From such a vantage point, the clones must have seemed small, almost ant-like. But this was how it was, and today, just like every other, everything seemed normal.

Yet it was not. One clone, a Packer called Ord, felt disoriented. He was finding it difficult to sort the boxes according to the new instructions. It was a small thing in itself – to stack them according to colours, categories and sizes. But it broke a habit of years. Ever since he had been transferred to the Hub, he had only ever stacked them according to weight – heaviest at the bottom, lightest at the top.

Ord stood nonplussed, as he thought how he, like the rest, had worked like robots and been praised for it. And wasn't that the whole point? They had to work like robots to prove that robots weren't needed. Or, at least, that's what they'd had drummed into them. But then, another thought sprang to the forefront of his mind: who am I to question? He hung his head in shame.

But the questioning began again as he knelt to check the colour, category and size of a box. He rubbed his left temple as if this might ease the speed at which thoughts sped pell-mell into his mind. It seemed to him that he could no longer be sure of anything anymore and that it was this change that had triggered it. He hardly knew how to put it, but only a few days after the new instructions had been introduced, his mind began to cloud. He had never experienced anything like it. He'd even had bouts of dizziness. Was it really the new routine? he wondered, biting the inside of his lower lip. Or was he just reacting badly to change? Slogan 32 said, 'No Change Is Good Change.' So why had they made this change? There! He was at it again – questioning. But, try as he might, he could not stop.

He wondered if his co-workers felt the same. Furtively, he glanced around. The nearest was Url. He was the one who had suggested the idea in the first place. Ord had thought nothing of it at the time Url had stood up and explained to the workgroup why he thought coding the boxes would be better. Judging by weight had led to too many mistakes, he had said. Ord had nodded his agreement like everyone else. But now, he felt confused.

He had tried to talk to Url about it, but he told him to bring it up at the next group meeting and added, pointedly, that private discussions were useless. Nonetheless, Ord asked others what they thought about it. None of them could understand why he found it so difficult to adjust to the change. He decided he had better not bring it up at the meeting. If he were the only one speaking out, he would risk distancing himself from the group. 'Individuality Divides,' he muttered, citing one of the most important slogans.

Instead, he had decided to submit a C80. It was the only option left. After all, he thought, this is what we're supposed to do when we can't talk about things in front of the group. Although he could not think of a single clone who had ever done this, he still thought it the safer course of action. It was less direct, less confrontational. The thought of standing up in front of the workgroup, to say nothing of the citizen-managers, to explain why he alone found the new rules so difficult... No, no, he shook his head, can't do that.

He had been steeling himself to the task all week, but each time he had found an excuse to delay. Pushing his fingers deep into his short-cropped, light brown hair, he told himself he would do it today. And yet he still dithered. He hated doing anything out of the ordinary. Didn't every packer? What was it the slogans said? Team First, Self Second? Or was it, 'Team is One, Self is None.' Good

Codes, he thought, shocked at how he could not recall this important slogan.

***

When the sound of chimes signalled the end of the shift, Ord pretended to be busy as co-workers headed for the changing rooms. When he judged it safe, he walked quickly, though not so fast as to draw attention, toward the massive column that housed the staircase and elevators that linked the Hub to the other floors of Joypolis Tower. As he approached, a door slid open. Entering, he glanced from side to side. Glad to see no one there, he began to jog down the spiral stairway since the elevators were reserved for citizen use only.

As he fretted about what he would say to the citizen clerks of the Secretarial Section, his pace slowed. How, he wondered, would they react? When his mind became a torrent of if-this then but if-not-that then, he stuttered to a stop. With one foot hovering over the lower step, he craned his neck upward. The glare from the electric light merely added an unwanted intensity to his indecision. It's no good, he thought, and was about to turn tail and run back up when, hearing footsteps, he froze.

He stood stock-still. To his amazement, a woman came into view. And what a beauty, he thought, his eyes widening.

She stopped in surprise and stared at him.

Ord turned and carried on down. He heard her footfalls follow his in a one-two beat. An A-class beauty for sure, he thought. He'd seen A-class beauties on the screens, but never in the flesh. He was wondering what she was doing here and why she wasn't using the elevators when the secretarial floor came into view. Panicking, he wondered if he should just stop, let her pass and then race back. He now felt as if he had been driven down by her.

Four more careful steps brought him level with a dark-tinted plastic door above which, in unadorned lettering, were the words 'Secretarial Section'. He stopped and stood with his back to the column that formed the centre of the stairwell waiting for the woman to pass. As she distanced herself from him, she triggered the door's sensors.

Two secretaries – a man and a woman – came into view. They were on the point of saying something, but froze on hearing the doors hiss open. The man smiled to the woman outside and raised five fingers to signal that he would be along shortly. The woman smiled back and pointed downward to indicate where she would be. As she sashayed past, Ord came into view. The man lowered his glasses and the woman cocked her head to one side. Ord took a deep breath and stepped forward.

He did not walk right up to them, but stopped short and bowed from the waist to indicate his lower rank. Glancing at the woman, the man raised an eyebrow.

'What is it?' he asked.

'I'd like a C80,' Ord croaked. He saw the man was about fifty and wore the high-soled footwear of the Director Class. He never dreamt he would come face to face with a director. He assumed it would be an ordinary citizen.

'You're a Packer, correct?'

'Yes,' Ord replied, knowing he had recognized his work category by the emblem on the breast pocket of his overalls. All clone personnel at the Hub came under the category Packer even if their duties were more specific. 'There's been a change in the stacking routine and... I'd like to say something about it,' he said, his voice petering out.

The woman touched the director's elbow so that he turned and she could whisper something in his ear. Facing Ord, the man asked, 'Have you discussed the matter with your workgroup?'

'No,' Ord gulped, beginning to feel hot. 'It doesn't seem to affect them. It's just me. I'm confused, that's why I came, you see, to follow the rules.' As he stared at his feet, he felt a bead of sweat trickling down his right temple.

The man conferred with the woman again. The man gave a sigh and the woman gestured Ord to follow.

She led him down a corridor at the end of which they turned and walked in front of a row of grey metal cabinets that housed hundreds of drawers labelled according to the forms they contained. She opened one and drew out a C80. It made a dry crackling sound when she flapped it and pointed Ord toward a solitary desk that stood in front of rows of banked desks. Once Ord was seated, she placed the form on the desk and withdrew.

Ord felt the stares of those sitting in the amphitheatre of desks behind drill their displeasure into his back. This wasn't how he imagined it would be. He felt as if he had been ordered to confess to a crime. It was all wrong. He thought his hand resemble a white crab as it slid across the desk toward the pen. No sooner had he taken it than he put it down to wipe his sweaty palms on his overalls. This done, he picked up the pen and began to write quickly, not because he had thought it through, but to get out of the place. It was hot, dry and stuffy. He hated it. He wrote:

I am confused. The new instructions for stacking the boxes, the new categories, codes, and colours for sorting, it makes my head ache. I feel dizzy, as if some sign had wormed its way into me. I am forgetting some of the slogans...

The Home Affairs Committee

The Home Affairs Committee was the most the influential of the several committees that governed Joypolis. As Chairman, Darvin sat at the head of the oval table around which the Directors of various government departments were seated. Everyone was present, except O, Director of Belief.

The main points of the meeting had already been covered and Gorvik, the Director of Cloning and Socialization, was explaining why he believed the Seventh article of the Clone Acts needed to be reformed. He was arguing for an amendment to allow for free cloning. He was in no mood to let the subject drop, despite sensing that Darvin was eager to bring the meeting to an end.

'The Seventh has outworn its usefulness and it's time we took a fresh look at this issue,' Gorvik repeated in a desperate bid to get his counterparts to move toward his position. 'We need intelligent clones, not an army of Low Personal Responders,' he said, looking into each face in the hope of detecting a sign of support. Finding none, he added darkly, 'It's time to change before change is forced upon us.'

'That sounds rather ominous,' rejoined Arron, Director of Administration. 'What do you mean "before change is forced upon us"? We have an affluent, stable society thanks to the wisdom and foresight of the Founders.' Arron knew this appeal to the semi-divine status of the Founders would elicit immediate support from the conservative members of the committee. Three of them duly nodded their heads.

'They knew more than any of us,' Arron continued, 'that the presence of LPRs would help the survivors. Having an underclass provides an important, psychological comfort. Don't you see, it helped the survivors to get through those difficult times, helped them overcome the terrifying sense of loneliness and isolation?'

'I'm not questioning the wisdom of the Founders,' Gorvik interrupted. 'I'm in as much awe of their vision as you. But that was two centuries ago. At that time, they were compelled to address the problem of how to secure the survival of a small number on a planet devastated by the impact of asteroids. There's no doubt that the introduction of a clone workforce created a brighter environment that pushed the birth rate problem to one side. And, I agree, it helped citizens come to terms with the harrowing fact that only Joypolis seems to have survived the catastrophe. But now, we have to address a different problem – stagnation. The presence of so many LPRs is having a detrimental effect on our citizens, especially the Manager Class. They show no initiative. They've become lazy and if we need to do something about it before it gets worse. What we need are creative scientific minds – of the very sort that made the Founders the kind of people they were. They never forbade change.'

'There's another aspect to this problem,' said Sovran, Director of Media. 'Recently, you may have heard that a child of seven died while being rushed to hospital. All of us know, and none more so than that poor child's mother, that we have the reproductive technology that could have re-created that child. The mother begged the paramedics to take samples of live tissue. They refused. In the end, she took some of her child's hair before he died...'

'Are you suggesting,' intervened the Chairman grimacing, 'that the Seventh be amended for resurrection cloning?'

'Yes. And if you'd interviewed that child's mother you would, too.'

'We can't make constitutional changes for a handful of people. For Code's sake, the person you're referring to could have another child naturally,' Darvin rasped.

'Please, please...' Gorvik said, raising a hand. 'I sympathize with my colleague and agree with her – resurrection cloning should be available in such tragic circumstances. But the real issue here is the subtle, cumulative effect of the undermining of the drive and motivation of our Manager Class.' Once more, Gorvik searched the faces around the table in the hope of finding support. 'It's the same insidious effect that servants have upon their masters. They un-man them. Look how the birth rate continues to fall. I believe there is a connection. Because we produce a clone labour force, it affects citizen reproduction. It has a knock-on effect of blunting the need for children. They don't feel they 'gain' from having children. In Darwinian terms, the 'cost' outweighs any advantage in terms of 'fitness'. It's another example of social inertia. This is the issue we need to address and its solution,' he hammered the table, 'is free cloning for intelligence.'

'There may be something in what Gorvik says about a decline in standards,' said Q'zar, Director of Security, his lean, bird-of-prey features turning to address the rest. 'I, too, sense a general malaise of sorts, especially among the young. But I don't know if you can blame it all on LPRs. I think a lot of responsibility lies with the tittle-tattle that Media bombards the citizens with day in and day out.'

Sovran shot a look of disdain at Q'zar. He was always carping on about the content of the news and other programmes. If he had his way, there would be twenty-four hours of propaganda every day of the year.

'But I would caution my colleague and any others who would dare tamper with the Seventh,' continued Q'zar, 'not to forget the Annals. The Story of–'

Before Q'zar could finish, Lara, Director of Education, jumped in to complete his sentence, 'Ore. How Ore married Freya and how, because neither were fertile, they decided to clone a daughter from Freya. And of how happy Ore was to see in Hera, their daughter, the image of his wife Freya.' Lara continued despite Gorvik raising a hand to intervene.

'If I've heard this once, I've heard it a thousand times...' Gorvik remonstrated, shaking his head.

'But as Freya grew older and Hera more beautiful, Ore began to lust after his own daughter until...' Lara went on, raising her voice in the face of Gorvik's protests.

'We know, we know – incest, genetic regression. For Code's sake, can't we get back to the point?' he pleaded.

'What I'm trying to say,' Lara shouted, 'is that's why the Seventh stipulates with golden clarity that a generation gap must be maintained. If donors knew who the clones were cloned from, we'd run the risk of incest and then, may the Founding Fathers protect us, we wouldn't know how to distinguish true human from artificial!'

'Has it never occurred to you,' Gorvik replied, 'that environment plays a big part in all of this? Hera would not have been like Freya. She would have grown up in a different society, had different experiences and been as different as you and Sovran,' he added, pointedly.

Before Gorvik could continue, Lara jumped up and shouted, 'The point of the myth isn't just about anonymity. It's about safeguarding what is truly human!' The last word was screamed into Gorvik's face.

Thinking he had better step in before the argument got any worse, Arron said, 'Ours is a small world and,' turning to face Gorvik, he added, 'I understand your enthusiasm for change and I applaud it. But this is different. I can't and won't mention the unspeakable, but everyone will understand when I say Joypolis is...an island.' Arron looked at each director in turn. It was as close as he could get to a subject that had become taboo – the Outside. Everyone inclined their heads, except Gorvik and Sovran.

It was Gorvik's view that fear of the Outside was part of the same problem – a dread that change could destabilise everything they had achieved. Knowing it was not a view he could gain any political advantage from, he remained silent though he was seething inwardly.

'I really must ask all of you to allow this meeting to move forward,' pronounced the Chairman, stepping into the fray. 'We seem, as usual, as far as this subject is concerned, to have reached an impasse. My view, after having taken careful note of what has been said, is that we need to have tangible evidence that our citizens are being weakened by the presence of so many clones as well as the claim that the fall in the birth rate is in some way connected to the same issue.

'I'm inclined to agree with the majority that the problem is not so pressing that we need to reform our sacred constitution. Even the seemingly innocuous amendment that Sovran has tried to persuade us of on humanitarian grounds would in my view open the floodgates. The inch that yields the yard, as the old proverb has it. Free cloning would, as the Founders saw, obscure traditional family relations and lead into a genetic quagmire.'

'What!' Gorvik burst out, unable to contain himself any longer. 'What are we, if not social engineers? Are we to become mere guardians of the past!'

'Order!' shouted Darvin. He did not like Gorvik's outburst one bit. They were becoming all too frequent. 'The matter is closed. Are we able to conclude this meeting or is there any other business?' he asked, drumming his fingers and looking only toward those he knew he could count upon for support. As no one spoke, he raised his head a fraction and was about to conclude the meeting when, crestfallen, someone spoke.

'Chairman, are you aware that a C80 has been submitted by a Packer?' asked Q'zar.

'Eh, no, I was not,' he replied, pulling the computer screen that he was on the point of closing up again. 'Does anyone know anything about this?' he asked in flat tones.

'Well, now, yes, yes, I believe I do,' replied Valchek who was Director of Personnel and effectively in charge of the entire clone workforce. 'Let's see, um, his files show he's the first and last of a batch of Ordinary Carer Clones, number C174, received into the Hub Warehouse exactly thirteen years, two months ago. What this means is that unlike other Packers who have benefited from the most up-to-date techniques of bio-semiotic conditioning, he, that is C174—'

'Yes, yes, we know all that,' Darvin snapped, 'but more to the point, why has he filed a C80?'

'I dare say he's entered the first stages of breakdown. He complains here,' Valchek said, pointing at a screen image of Ord's C80, 'of a change in his routine. It's the usual symptoms – fussing about some trivial matter. He's the last of that model and, frankly, I'm surprised he's lasted this long. Our modern models have all the refinements and advantages of modern coding...'

'So what do we do with him?' broke in the Chairman, flexing his fingers in front of his bushy eyebrows.

Thinking that he might be able to get the last word in on the issue of free cloning, Gorvik spoke up.

'This may not be entirely relevant, but I think it's worth mentioning that this Carer became a Packer, something that was not intended. I remember there were others and they've already deconstructed. This kind of situation doesn't arise very often, but some of you may recall that we had a similar situation a few weeks ago, discussed at a different meeting. Thirty-odd female Carers were transferred to the Aesthetics School to work as Sex Servicers.'

Arron nodded while Valchek looked on uneasily as Gorvik continued: 'We really ought to avoid this kind of situation. We condition them for one task and then, because of some bureaucratic mix-up, they're assigned to an entirely different one! That's why they deconstruct earlier than they should. It's not profitable.'

'It's not easy to predict exact ratios of supply and demand for all the different work categories,' Arron replied. 'We do our best but, well, there are occasions when we get it wrong. Statistically speaking, it's a very small number.'

'Does this matter?' Darvin asked, puzzled at their concern.

'Well,' replied Gorvik, 'this situation certainly wouldn't exist if free cloning were introduced.'

'That subject is closed,' Darvin snapped, turning red in the face.

Valchek was the first to break the awkward silence that followed. 'As a rule,' he said, 'we let them deconstruct so that their peers can witness their anti-social behaviour before they're taken to the Encrypt.'

Q'zar, whose hooded eyes had not left Valchek for an instant, said, 'Doesn't he complain of a new arrangement of the boxes, a new system being introduced?'

'Yes,' said Valchek, scrolling down Ord's file. 'He does say something of that sort, but the crux of the matter is the change in his routine coupled with his age and, above all, that he belongs to our...'

'...earlier more primitive clones,' the Chairman chimed in. 'Now, we really must bring this meeting to a close. Time is pressing. Q'zar, are you satisfied this clone poses no threat to security and can be left to decline like the rest of his batch?'

'Yes,' replied Q'zar, concealing his contempt for the true reason behind the Chairman's haste to bring the meeting to an end. He couldn't wait to see his beloved Zuriko Azari.

'If that's the case,' the Chairman said, without looking around the table, 'this meeting is concluded.' He then rose from his chair and began gathering papers and putting them into a folder as quickly as he could, ignoring Valchek who was still muttering.

'Of course, he does complain of a sign...' Valchek mumbled, before looking up and noticing everyone was getting ready to leave.

Silver Lines

Ord heaved a sigh of relief as the door of the changing room clanged shut behind him. No one was there. He was glad. He did not want to talk to anyone. Walking along a row of metal lockers, he came to his own. He didn't need to check its number: he knew it from the habit of years. He let his forehead fall and rest against its cool surface. Codes, he thought, what's coming down?

After a while, he yanked the door open, pulled his overalls off and changed into beige chinos and a blue cotton jerkin. He was about to close the locker door when he caught sight of his image in the mirror behind it. Those lines around my mouth are getting so deep they're making me look like a monkey, he thought. Seeing a frightened look in his eyes, he wondered, who am I?

Pushing the locker shut, he walked toward the door at the far end of the changing room. It slid open at his approach. He walked through and, head bowed, began to climb the stairs to the ground floor.

Reaching the spacious atrium of the ground floor of the Tower, he weaved his way through the crowd to a silver-line walkway. All clone walkways were silver lines. He joined the line waiting to step onto it. As he stepped onto its slow, gliding floor, clones were pushing past him. This is more like it, he thought, just a face in the crowd. He took several deep breaths as the tube within which the walkway glided left the Tower. The air of the surface always felt good after a day's work beneath ground.

Looking out, he could see other tubular walkways above and below. Wherever a clone silver line ran parallel to a citizen gold line, there was partitioning. Ord wondered why. He supposed they did not want citizens and clones seeing one another outside of work. He looked up at one of the many screens that hung from above when he noticed The News come on. He tried to catch what was being said, but it was difficult to hear against a background of announcements warning them not to run, not to place luggage on the belts, not to forget any belongings and not to leave litter.

As the walkway became more crowded, Ord wondered why the silver lines were not wider. After all, there were far more clones than citizens. They outnumbered them three to one. The citizen walkways were almost empty. The thought sparked a sad memory. He remembered Krm.

Krm had worked at the Hub until last year. Ord wanted to help him, but in the end group pressure proved too strong. Krm had to be forcibly removed from the workgroup session. He was screaming, 'We're human, too. You put those slogans in our heads, you take them out. They're not ours, they're yours. Your lies, not ours... yours, yours, yours!'

It was the saddest moment of his life to see Krm dragged out of the room yelling and hollering like that. True, what he'd done a couple of weeks ago had been out of the ordinary. But handing in a C80 was following the rules. Krm had been removed because he'd gone individ and become violent. That's why they'd taken him to the

Encrypt. No one was allowed to visit the Encrypt and no one ever returned to work from there. He hoped they were looking after him. It still hurt. Krm was his twin.

Ord gazed down at the streets. It was already dark and, in the distance, he could see the neon-lit district he was gliding toward. He twisted his head from side to side. Codes, I'm stiff, he thought. Need a massage. He wondered if the strain was getting to him: Krm and the slogans, me and the new sorting instructions. Of course, we are all human, he thought and wondered why Krm could think that they weren't. He looked at the silhouettes of a group of citizens on a gold line going in the opposite direction. What could be so different? Alright, they never met socially. But he doubted they could be so different that...they were less human. He ran through some of the obvious differences: citizens lived longer and some had children. Clones had to get permission for children. But no one did and that's why no one felt any resentment. So why did Krm go individ?

As he was carried along, advertisements floated in and out of his vision. Most were eye-catching posters of products, places and events. Others were animated and displayed on screens. But here and there, slogans were flashed by a deep red pulsing light. Ord had just passed one and, though he'd not noticed it, the word 'harmony' came to mind. 'We're all Joypolitans,' he murmured.

Stepping off the walkway, he walked down to the main drag of the Pink Zone. He stood looking around as crowds swirled past. In the distance, he could see the myriad lights of Joypolis Tower scintillating between highrise buildings. Here, however, it was very different. The buildings were jumbled together. Ord looked at the tops of a line of pillars that had once supported a huge bio-dome. Not all of them were visible, some were concealed by buildings. They were a relic of the past. He didn't know why, but he liked them. Perhaps it was their unusualness or uselessness, he thought as he turned into a labyrinth of small alleys.

As he walked past bars, eating houses, sex parlours, kiosks for stimulants and game houses, the smell of cooking made him hungry. He dived into a single-room restaurant, squeezed himself up onto an empty stool at the counter and ordered a bowl of noodles and steamed Chinese dumplings. As he waited, he noticed the restaurant was backed up against a section of an old pillar. He supposed these massive structures had been left because it would have been more trouble to tear them down.

Soon, a bowl of noodles was handed to him over the counter. Ord wasted no time tucking in. As he slurped the noodles up, the dumplings were slipped past his elbow onto the counter. Ten minutes later, he was outside wiping his lips with the back of his hand wondering what to do and which way to go.

As he looked up and down the narrow lane, a girl wearing hot pants and a pink plastic cape came up and handed him a leaflet. He looked at it. It read: 'Discounts! Discounts! Look at these prices! Oil massage only 500 Jcs!' As he looked at the pictures of the girls on the back, the girl smiled and said, 'If you come now, I'll do you.' Ord noticed she had a perfect row of white teeth. 'It's the best place in town. Everybody says so. No messing about.'

Ord looked her up and down. Her cape reached the hem of her hot pants. He saw her legs were big at the top, but not fat. Her hair was the most striking thing about her. She had it fanned out onto a frame with fairy lights going on and off. What a get-out, he thought. He judged her to be about twenty-five, although she could have been older. It was difficult to tell, her face so caked with make-up.

'Haven't seen you before,' he said, surprised at how he could have missed anyone so conspicuous in a district he frequented so often.

'Eva,' she said, wriggling her shoulders to better display her headdress. 'I'm new.'

Ord wasn't sure if she had said Eve, Eva, or Emma because someone had just come out of a Game Booth and the roar of machines had drowned her voice.

'Whatever,' he said, letting her take his wrist and lead him toward a purple door shaped like a keyhole. He thought he would have the regular course, then go and have a drink with Srl and Tor and try to stop thinking about when the secretaries would reply to his C80.

When Eva shut the door behind them, the racket outside was silenced as abruptly as if a switch had been thrown. It made the narrow foyer of the parlour seem strangely peaceful. Eva pointed to a man who sat at a desk behind a plastic screen with holes in it. At the same time, another man who had been sitting at the bottom of the stairs got up and gave Eva a tap on the ass as he passed her. With smoke curling out of his mouth, he pointed to the tariffs and asked Ord what course he would like.

Ord replied the regular, dug deep into his pockets and paid the man who sat behind the plastic screen. He followed Eva up the creaky stairs. As he did so, he noticed a small battery attached to the clasp at the back of her choke. So that's how she does the fairy lights, he thought. Suddenly dizzy, he grabbed hold of the banister. As he closed his eyes, Krm's face appeared.

'Come on,' Eva called from the top of the stairs. 'You've only got thirty minutes.'

Ord looked up. She was standing, legs apart, golden hair lit up. She reminded him of a cartoon character called Sammy Sunrise. Sammy's hair was fanned out like that, too. Not bedecked with lights, but like black flames. Sammy used to help kids when things went wrong. Like if a friend was going individ. Shakily, Ord pulled himself up the stairs wondering if he was ill.

Eva led him to a room at the end of an uneven passage. Entering, they undressed and got into a shower. She began to soap him down. Ord knew it was the risk of disease that made the servicers scrub their customers so well, but even so he wondered if she weren't deliberately wasting time.

'It's okay,' he said in all earnestness. 'You don't have to lick my ass.'

She stopped, showered the soap off him and began to rub him down with a towel. When he was dry, she led him to a bed with a mirror above. Eva adjusted the lighting to a dim red and asked him the usual questions: did he want it this way or that as she ran her hands over him and pushed her breasts into his face. He told her to suck him off first and then give him a massage.

After a few minutes, he knew something was wrong. He eased her off and looked around for his clothes. 'Forget it. Uh, doesn't matter,' he muttered as he pulled his pants on. Looking at his limp cock, he thought that's never happened before. Maybe I am ill, he thought.

'You a Packer?' Eva asked, thinking to fill in the time with small talk.

'Yeah, but I wasn't trained as one. I'm a Carer. I was transferred to the Hub. I been working there so long, I guess you could say I'm a Packer. No different from anyone else there. Yep, I'm a Packer.' As he pulled his shirt on, he felt glad of the momentary darkness.

Eva said quietly, 'That's odd. 'Cos I'm not a servicer, either. I was a Carer. Only three months ago. Bringing up kids, I was, till they said something about not needing so many and there being a shortage of servicers 'n all. Can't say I like it much. I was trained as a Carer. Liked that. Liked it a lot, I did.'

Ord looked at her sideways up as he buckled his belt. 'You, a Carer? Must be... kind of difficult... this work?'

Eva met his gaze full on and held it without saying anything. Ord wondered what that look meant as he looked away and said, 'I... I filled in a ...C80...couple of weeks ago, it was.' There was no answer. He carried on, gazing past her, telling her about the change in his routine, how confusing it was, how unnecessary, how he thought he had to do something about it. He did, submitted a C80, better that than bringing it up at the meeting, especially as no one in the group seemed to know what he was on about. He'd gone to the secretaries, met a director, didn't think that would happen, and what with the way he was remembering Krm, his twin, everything coming back, like at the least expected moment. Why, just few minutes ago on the stairs, he wasn't feeling too well, not his usual self. Wasn't like this; usually he could come, no problem. Catching himself, he wondered how long he had been rabbiting on when a buzzer sounded. 'Sorry, I... uh.'

Eva looked toward the sound and back at Ord. He looked at her and shrugged his shoulders. She began to dress. When she finished, she asked, 'You got everything?' Ord nodded.

As they left the room, Eva whispered, 'Don't say anything to...will you?' She pointed to the floor below, meaning, he supposed, the guy downstairs. Ord nodded. As he turned into the passage, she touched him lightly on the side of his arm. He was not sure what that touch meant and turned to look at her. He saw her smile. It wasn't the same smile as before. It was different. He was trying to put a word to it, or so he would think later, when it vanished and they retraced their steps to the foyer.

As he walked toward the door, the man who was smoking, got up and thanked him for his custom and said they looked forward to his next visit.

Stepping out into the jangling confusion of the street, Ord set off in the direction of the bar he thought Srl and Tor would be at. As he did so, he mumbled under his breath: 'Phew, better not mention this one to the boys.' He had not gone far when he stopped and held his head. It was throbbing. He decided to go home. He had had enough for one day.

The Alzaris

At the conclusion of yet another meeting, Arron, the Director of Administration and the same person Ord had met on submitting a C80, decided to visit his favourite club, the Alzaris. It was one of the most exclusive, but, unlike so many of the new members, Arron did not go there to rub shoulders with names. He liked it for its calm, unchanging atmosphere. As he grew older, it seemed to him that Joypolitan society was becoming ever more desperate in its search for novelty. Why can't they leave things as they are? he wondered as he stepped into an elevator.

As it soared upward, he tried to clear his mind of the clutter of impressions left by the meeting. Gorvik was not going to give up – he was determined to get the Seventh amended. If he could, he'd have it repealed, never mind amended. Can't see it happening though. Not as long as Darvin's in the chair. Sovran seems to be moving in Gorvik's direction. Lara will never endorse it. Neither will Q'zar. The question is, will Valchek? He's probably biding his time, waiting to get the highest price for his allegiance, never mind the issue. Darvin's going to need more than political cunning if Gorvik and Sovran join forces. He'll need a strong argument – something he sadly lacks.

Alighting at the next floor but one from the top of Joypolis Tower, Arron was met by Georg, the club's major domo. He extended his hand for Arron's cape. Arron unclipped it, handed it him, and followed him into the club. Georg swung the cape with a practised flourish over his forearm and led him as if they were entering the court of a foreign king. Arron wondered what it was about this man that made him do everything, even the smallest of tasks, as if they were all of such momentous importance.

As they entered, he looked around and noticed with satisfaction that the club was, just as he had hoped, almost empty. There were only two guests and they were about as far away from his customary seat as possible. When he sat down, Georg asked if he required 'his usual' and withdrew at his nod. Recently, some members had taken to calling him by his name. Arron considered this far too friendly. Turning, he gazed out of the window to change this fruitless line of thought.

Had he not seen this view countless times, it would have left him breathless. At a hundred and eighteen metres high, the view was magnificent. As he rested his eyes upon the green patchwork of the forest rolling into the distance, he settled back into his armchair and thought of Laia. He felt so happy. Laia, the very courtesan Ord had encountered on his way to the Secretariat, had agreed to become his official consort. He remembered how he'd fretted before popping the question. He was terrified she might refuse. Praise the Codes, he thought. He did not want to go through all that again.

He had liked her right from the start – the very first time he had set eyes upon her. He pictured the scene again. 'Yes,' she'd said, 'Yes.' And all this happiness was because of that yes. The relief he'd felt was overwhelming. He felt as if his head were in the clouds. Or, at least, as close to passion as a man of his age and temperament could be. As the joy subsided, a warm afterglow had filled him. This, he thought, is much better: it can be savoured. He took a sip of claret and, realizing he'd not even noticed Georg put it there, took a quick look around before returning to his reverie.

At the beginning, he did not think he had a chance. All right, he had the status and, in one sense, he could have almost anybody he wanted. But for a consort and a civic ceremony he wanted someone for whom he felt something special. Of course, he'd met other courtesans, but their charm seemed artificial. Flatterers, the lot of them he thought. But Laia, she had it all – youth, beauty, and that extra something that he couldn't put his finger on, but which made everything so complete. For him, it wasn't just her natural charm and beauty, it was the quality of feeling she brought to their relationship. She created the most marvellously intimate atmospheres, the like of which he'd never experienced before. I adore her, he thought. I'm in love!

He'd worried that she might refuse because of his age. She was only twenty-four and he fifty-six. But she didn't seem to mind. He actually believed she should mind. Or, at least, at first he did. But when he realized his age did not enter her reckoning, it mattered less and less. At one point, he wondered if he weren't being selfish: robbing her of a more robust relationship. But gradually, he realized why his age did not matter: she had never known her father. But what did it matter if he were a father-substitute if it did not affect the quality of their love?

No, she had been too young to remember her father. Not only he, but everyone knew this. Her father had been involved in the crime of the century. Alex Drovny was his name. He and her mother, Pharo, were partners. Social media was full of gossip about them. They often appeared on television, talking about what they liked to eat and whether they would ever live together and so on. They were very happy. But Drovny was also desired by the wealthy Azari. She craved him as her gamete partner and was not one to be denied. She arranged to meet Pharo on the pretext of having her horoscope done. Pharo, unaware of her true motive, kept the appointment. It was her last. After weeks of searching, her body was found rotting on the outskirts of the city. She had been stabbed to death. When investigators, at Drovny's prompting, started questioning Azari, she denied the charges. But when the murder weapon was found, the evidence was stacked against her. A formal charge was delayed because of her position and influence. At one point, it looked as if she might even get away with it. Incensed, Drovny broke into her apartment, strangled her and committed suicide.

According to Q'zar, the excitement whipped up by Media played no small part in the bungling of the investigation by his department. Eventually, he managed to marshal political support and put pressure on Media to shift its focus to other matters. Lee, who then headed Media, reluctantly agreed. Gradually, the whole matter was consigned to history. All three became icons of the pitfalls of passion and the affair dubbed the Romeo Complex. In short, it was explained away.

In the aftermath, one of the recommendations was that Pharo and Azari's daughters, Laia and Zarina (renamed Zuriko) should be fostered within the School of Aesthetics so that the karma of their past should not be revisited upon them. Karma, indeed, scoffed Arron. But he had to admit that, in this case at least, the recommendation had proven successful. Neither Laia nor Zuriko seemed to bear one another any grudge and both had grown up as psychologically normal.

He believed his reputation was in the clear. Drovny's suicide had proved he was innocent, Laia was much liked and Zuriko hugely popular. No doubt when they declared their civic union, some political enemies might try to sully his reputation. And, yes, he supposed he would run the risk of losing face. But the impression he'd got from sounding out a number of influential figures was positive. Some even hinted that he might gain from such a union. He did not like the insinuation of altruism for political gain, but he'd thought about it very carefully and believed his gain in terms of happiness far outweighed any possible, temporary loss of face.

At this point, Arron's reverie was interrupted by laughter from a group of people entering the club. He leaned over and saw Sovran leading them. Tall, black, and with features so arresting one could easily imagine she was an archetype of her race. She certainly had charisma, and though one could hardly fault her for that, Arron knew this gave her an uncanny gift of getting people to talk far more than was good for them. He eased himself back into his armchair. After a few moments, he heard their chatter subside as they moved away. He stole one more glance in their direction to see where they had sat. That's where O used to sit, he thought.

Recently, he had noticed an article in the *Joypolitan Times*. It was a satire of O's Belief Department. No doubt Sovran was behind it. It was not a lead story or anything like that. That would have been too risky. It was an on-going raillery of an inefficient government department. Different names had been used to avoid political repercussions, but it was clearly ridiculing O and his department.

Hardly surprising, Arron had to admit. O had neither been seen nor heard of for almost five years. As a result, both the department as well as O had become a laughing stock. But for the fact that O was a direct descendant of Dovan, the leader of the Founders, criticism would have been far less muted.

Originally, O's department had been established to provide citizens with an alternative to religion which was considered subversive. But O's teachings had become more and more divorced from mainstream thinking which was utilitarian. O was not his real name, but one he had chosen as symbolising his belief in the contemplation of the void. He no longer lived on the Topround of the Tower with Joypolis' elite, but wandered the streets like an itinerant. While most citizens considered him eccentric, the reaction of the nobility ranged from embarrassment to outright condemnation. No one knew exactly where he lived. Security could easily find out, but O's privileged position forbade them from doing so. It would have been 'bad form'.

Arron's rumination on O's withdrawal from public life were interrupted by another group entering the club. This time they sat within earshot, something he could not abide. Not wishing to make it plain that he was leaving because of their presence, he lingered and watched how the wild ground between the trees at the edge of the forest and the city's perimeter was being levelled to provide landfill sites. May the Will of the Founders protect us from the Outside, he murmured before draining his glass and heading for the exit.

AT HOME

Ord's room was on the second floor of a two-floor dormitory located in Clone District 5. It stood near the perimeter. The room was small and sparsely furnished and had only one window – a pair of sliding glass doors that opened onto a narrow veranda which was used for hanging clothes out to dry. Ord stood behind the doors watching the sun set. He wondered why he had begun to enjoy watching the sun rise and fall. He did not know, but every evening when he got back from the Hub he would find himself at this window watching that great orb sink. He supposed he found it relaxing. The way the colours changed and, even when darkness fell, he marvelled at how sudden it was. He could not decide whether the darkness rose or fell. Perhaps it was like a net of tiny black points getting larger until they blotted everything out. Whatever, it didn't matter. It was beautiful. He raised his head a fraction to view the saffron mantle that spilled over the treetops.

    He wondered why he had never noticed all this before. He supposed, he'd had no need to then. Then, he wasn't ill. Before, he would have been out with co-workers – eating, drinking, playing at the game centres, going to the sex parlours, just being himself. But since the headaches began, he found the noise, smoke, drink, confusion and crowds unbearable. Now he preferred to be on his own. He found it calmed him to watch the sky shift through an ever-softening spectrum of colour. Even the trees grew stiller, he thought, noticing how they had stopped swaying.

Two months had passed since he had submitted the C80 and he'd heard nothing. He had carried on working, doing his best. But everything felt different. He was becoming more and more conscious of things that he'd never paid any attention to before. It was like he was seeing the Hub differently. Noticing its smells, sounds and even stopping to feel the texture of the boxes he was stacking. Everything was getting...he wasn't sure there was a word for it... closer, more real? Before, he just did everything without thinking. Now he felt there was an edge to everything.

He had lost his temper. That was four days ago. It was a small matter, but he'd been led off the Hub floor. It didn't involve anyone else, thank the Codes. He lowered his head in shame. He'd hurled a box. Didn't know what had come over him. He was kicking it when the restraining hand of a security guard brought him back to his senses.

He wondered if the authorities would let it go by. He'd been taken to a manager's office, told to take a seat, handed a glass of water and asked if he felt all right. He thought they'd really tear into him, give him a lecture or make him recite the first ten slogans. But no, they accepted his apologies. In fact, they were very kind. That was when he'd mentioned the C80 to them. They said they knew nothing about that, but assured him they'd look into it. They said he'd probably get a reply soon. They told him to take the rest of the day off and relax. They'd let him know when to come back. Everybody had been so kind.

But he'd still not heard from them. Surely they wouldn't...
No, he mused, brushing the thought aside.

As darkness fell, a strange thought made him straighten up. He wondered what it was like...Out there. Codes, why am I thinking such a thing? He shook his head. They'd been told never to cross the perimeter and, as far as he knew, no one had. Who'd want to anyway? It was dangerous. Everybody knew that. And yet, the stillness... it all seemed so... peaceful.

Ord turned away from his ghostly reflection and looked around the room. He wondered if he would ever get a bigger one. He'd heard some clones had been rewarded for their years of service. He'd never actually met one. He supposed he would forfeit any reward after what had happened at work. He was still young, only 34, he thought. Perhaps, he could make up for it.

Sighing, he sat on the sofa and pushed a button on the home automation console that was built into its arm. A large picture materialised on a screen that filled the entire wall. He flipped through some entertainment channels till he reached the multimedia encyclopaedia he was searching for. He set the search at random and waited for all the crazy things that such a search usually threw up.

The first find was about 'Odin'. He listened to a narration of his place among the gods of a primitive militant religion and how the invocation of his name inspired the Goths and other warlike tribes to fight so fiercely that a powerful empire fell and an age of chaos ensued. Amazing, he thought, as he looked at the virtual images of these warriors. They'd be no good at the Hub, he concluded, in an effort to cheer himself up.

The next find was 'marriage'. This was described as a social union blessed by religious orders. How ridiculous, he thought, not to say unnatural, cruel and perverted –

to bind healthy people by law to one partner. Although, on reflection, he thought it was not unlike the consort system practised by nobles and directors. While citizens were encouraged to bank their sperm or eggs at a young age in case they wanted children, the nobles and directors rarely did so. Most men opted for a vasectomy to avoid incurring the cost of abortions. He'd heard that some women opted to have their oviducts blocked. Later, if a couple wanted to have a baby they would arrange to have the gametes of their banked sperm and eggs united. But even then, they did not live together. They might, but not in the way marriage was described. The law was not about keeping partners together but protecting mothers and children financially.

Feeling his head begin to tire, he stopped the search and began to think about calling up a sex servicer. He'd not been feeling much like having sex recently. It was unusual. He enjoyed his sex and spent most of his wage on sex play just like other clones. He toyed with the telecom, but let it drop. Listlessly, he pushed the console button again and flicked it to The News show.

As he watched, Ord was unaware that he also was being observed. The Security Department had ordered the activation of a small device installed in the upper corner of his screen. All screens had this 'eye', though not all were activated. In fact, it would have been impossible for the Security Department to observe every clone at the same time because its personnel were too few. In any case, there had never been an occasion when more than a few clones needed to be observed simultaneously. But now, far away, in an empty room of the Security Department, an image of Ord's pale face flickered on a screen which would be viewed at a later, more convenient time.

Ord suddenly sat bolt upright when a newscaster began to report an incident at the Hub. 'There was an ugly incident at the Hub some days ago. A clone had to be dragged off to a safe room. And what do they have to say about this at the Hub? We're going live: here's John Truman at the Hub with an on-the-spot interview with Packer Manager Ying Huang.' The manager's face appeared but no interviewer could be seen.

'Huang, News has it that a Packer went berserk and had to be bundled into a safe room. Is this true?'

'Well, there was a disturbance and, naturally, that's to be regretted. But I'd like to stress that one bad apple shouldn't be taken as a reflection of our workforce.' Huang frowned. 'In fact, morale has never been higher. 'Deeds not Words' is our motto.'

'Will he be back to work tomorrow?'

'He has been asked to rest.'

'Was he reprimanded?'

'He agreed to rest.'

'Do you plan to take any further action?'

'No comment.'

'Will he be junked?'

'That's not our decision.'

The picture cut back to the studio.

'Thank you, John. And now we have a report coming in on the big match...'

Ord felt stunned. His eyes bulged as he stared ahead seeing nothing. His head began to spin as a riot of thoughts clamoured for attention. Unable to bear it, he pulled his head down between his knees. In an agony of shame, he wondered, would they? Could they junk him? Unable to bear the cramped space of his room anymore, he rushed out.

Once he stepped out onto the street, he began to run to burn off energy. When he finally came to a gasping stop he was surprised to find himself beside the perimeter. He could hear the wind soughing through the trees that stood only fifty metres away on the other side of a stretch of open ground. He waited till he stopped panting before turning back. All the way, he was tormented by the thought that they would come and take him, as they had Krm, to the Encrypt.

When he got back, he threw himself onto the bed. No sooner had he done so than he felt his head begin to throb with pain. He groaned as he twisted from side to side unable to sleep.

THE CHAIRMAN

Zuriko dabbed the final touches to her make-up. Looking one way and then another, she felt satisfied. Her coal-black eyes were radiant and she knew, with a mere flutter, they could entice. Right now, they were smoky and had a lazy leonine look about them. She smiled to herself as she put the mascara brush back into its case and snapped it shut. Yes, she thought, I have done rather well to have climbed this high, to have Darvin as my... Pausing, she took a pearl necklace from an enamelled box and lifted it into the light to admire. Yes, she surmised, picking up the thread of her thought, as my source of information. Just then, a tap at the door made her turn.

A maid popped her head round and whispered, 'It's the Chairman. I've kept him waiting as you said.'

'I'll meet him now. You may go.' Zuriko took one last look at her jet-black hair which was cut square at the front to emphasize the perfect balance and proportion of her face. Satisfied, she rose and went through the adjoining room to the spacious reception room in which Darvin waited with his hands behind his back, looking out of a window.

Hearing her, Darvin swung round and beamed at her beauty. 'Why Zuriko, it hardly seems possible, but you look even more ravishing than when we last met.'

'Ah, more flattery,' Zuriko replied, laughing as she took his hand.

'I have a little something for you,' continued Darvin, taking a small gift box from out of his jacket pocket.

'Oh, you're too kind! Just put it there.' She pointed to a low marble-topped table, 'And help me with this, will you?' She spun round and held the ends of the pearl necklace he'd given her. 'Could you fasten it, Dee-dee?'

'Of course, I shall my Z and I do so like it when you call me 'D'.' He took the proffered ends, noticing as he did so how she had painted her nails purple. His favourite colour. As he linked the necklace, he inhaled the fragrance of her perfume and let his eye run down the alluring line of her neck. Involuntarily, a sigh of satisfaction escaped him. Instantly, Zuriko sprang away, sensing he was on the point of kissing her bare shoulders.

'And what would my illustrious D like to have...' she said and added coquettishly, '...to drink?'

Darvin smiled. How he loved her little games! He sat on the sofa, relishing the delicate pastel shades of pink and pale blue that suffused the room. 'Oh, let me think,' he said as nonchalantly as he could, 'a dusk-bomb, my Zee-zee.'

'A dusk-bomb,' she said, impressed, 'and what has my Dee-dee been doing today to so-so need a big-big dusk-bomb?'

'Ahh, the corridors of power,' Darvin answered with practised weariness. 'But I'm afraid I shall only bore you my beautiful, and ever more beautiful, Zee-zee.'

'No, no, tell me,' Zuriko persisted, handing him his drink in a tall stemmed glass. 'I do so love to listen to Dee-dee's twoubles.' She pouted like a baby. 'And, besides, when I've heard your twials and twibulations, I shall know exactly how you'll want me... and have me... later,' she added, letting her forefinger glance his lips.

After glugging a large draught, Darvin put the glass down with a sigh of satisfaction.

'I do so love my time with you,' he said. 'If I seem old and tired at times, can you forgive me?'

Zuriko went and sat beside him. Snuggling up, she murmured, 'What's twoubling my Dee-dee?'

'Oh, it's Gorvik. He's pressing to have the Clone Laws reformed. It's dangerous. But he's persuasive and some are beginning to listen. And we have a clone deconstructing,' he began wearily, 'not that there's anything new about that, but Q'zar – yes, him again – he thinks there's more to it than Valchek's letting on. He's got the clone under observation. He thinks someone might be introducing subversive signs! The man is completely paranoid. Valchek couldn't hatch a plot if he tried. He's an egg-head, for Code's sake!'

'There, there,' soothed Zuriko, getting up and going behind him to massage his shoulders. 'But Dee-dee, what in the world is a subversive sign? How can there be such a thing? The Illustrious Codes forbid such signs, don't they?'

'Well, I probably, no correction, certainly shouldn't be telling you this,' he said, squirming, but now so fully ensconced in Zuriko's aura of annihilating sweetness that he was unable to check himself. 'The Codes were based on a discovery of a group of genes in the left perisylvian region of the brain. They control the transmission of messages, and, well, once the chemical processes involved in their transmission were understood, bio-semioticians put their heads together and designed a program that became the blueprint for the conditioning of the clones.'

'The peri- what! How do you know all this D!' cried Zuriko.

Darvin laughed, 'The peri-whatever-you-like darling. Gorvik and the boffins have all the details, but that blueprint and its approved signs define the range of variation open to clone consciousness. It's this that Gorvik wants changed. He's saying the Seventh is no longer needed and should be scrapped. Scrap this, scrap that! Scrap indoctrination, scrap the generation rule... Codes, he'd scrap everything if he had his way! But, where was I? Ah yes, it was clear from the start that bio-semioticians could, if there weren't controls in place, create clones other than those approved by the Clone Laws. How? By introducing subversive signs. Highly unlikely, but Q'zar – he who trusts no one – says the clone complained of a sign. So what! The clone's going gaga! He could be dreaming of unicorns for all we know! As usual, Q'zar's blowing it out of all proportion. He's also insisting we find out where the new instructions for sorting the warehouse goods came from. Can you believe it! Check this, check that, check everything!'

'He's horrible. None of my girls like him. They say he's as cold as the...' Zuriko gestured toward the unmentionable Outside. 'But it's only one clone, isn't it, Dee-dee? So, it's nothing to worry about.' She went and took his empty glass from his hand and placed it upon the table so as to sit astride his lap. She kissed his balding head, knowing full well that Darvin could never resist her breasts so close.

'Yes, only one,' she heard him say a jot unsteadily, 'and only one of an early type. Valchek says he'll find out where the new instructions came from, says it was another clone's idea. I doubt if any of the newer batches will deconstruct. If they did, Gorvik would have more ammunition for free cloning, um...'

Zuriko drew his head against her breasts as the thought crossed her mind that, perhaps, something was afoot, a power struggle even. The thought of any change that might threaten her position as Head of the Aesthetics School made her eyes narrow.

Looking down, she slipped a shoulder strap off lest Darvin pull her dress out of shape. This is how I shall keep him, she thought. Until...

For Zuriko, having the Chairman as her consort and all the information that she could extract from him was not the pinnacle of her ambition. There was another matter that made her dig her nails into his back.

She scarcely noticed his squeal of pain as she recalled the first time she had learnt the importance of information. It was by pure chance. Though now, with hindsight, she believed it was fate. She was a young pupil of the Aesthetics School. The class had been told the lesson was over and they could go and play. The teacher had to speak to the Principal. She had hardly left the classroom when she realized she had forgotten her Kitty box and dashed back to get it. She was on the point of rushing into the classroom when she heard her name mentioned. She stopped in her tracks and listened unseen. As she listened, the blood drained from her face. '...Zuriko and Laia get on so well, truly like sisters. Of course, they have their little tiffs, but like the rest, they always make up. No one would think her mother had been murdered by Laia's father...' Gulping back a bewildering confusion of feelings, she crept away. When the day ended and she returned to her room, she collapsed in a heap and fell into a confused sleep.

On waking, she did not know what to do. Although she longed to know the truth, she decided to wait before deciding what to do. It turned out she did not need to wait long. They were summoned to the Principal's office so that the whole matter could be explained to them. It was important, it seemed, that they heard the 'right' version – a version so watered down that it made their parents out to be fools. They were told to accept this and look to the future. Even now, it angered her to think how stupid the Principal's story was. It was an insult. Her mother had been murdered before she could prove her innocence! And Drovny's suicide had nothing to do with remorse – he was guilty of both murders. How Laia could have been so gullible to believe the Principal, she would never know.

She hated Laia. True, while young, they'd been like sisters. But when their adult selves began to emerge they became opposites. After graduating, Laia had chosen to enter the ranks of courtesans and they had little contact. Zuriko smiled to think how much better she had fared. She had risen to head the School and was in charge of the sex industry – Sex Friends for citizens and Sex Servicers for clones. She had worked hard at changing the image of the School to one of fun, enjoyment, therapy and health. Originally, it had been founded to provide an open sex service to rid society of sexually motivated crime. However, the demand of certain customers for certain men or women had introduced the notion of value. Payment became the only means for resolving this source of contention. Very quickly, the service became a financial enterprise and, equally quickly, there were several scandals concerning the huge profits being made. The new image she had worked to create had helped conceal the scale of the profits. Of course, there were limits to her power, but thanks to her wealth she was able to bribe well-placed individuals for information. In this way, she had got wind of Arron's intention to make Laia his consort. It offered Laia a safe haven. She had to stop it and quickly. But how?

As she watched Darvin struggling out of his jacket, her eyes lit up with an idea. I'll find out more about this clone. Warton'll help, she thought. Warton was a Watcher who had been selling her information for better sex friends. Pity he's so rough with the girls, she thought. Still, I'll play him along. Delighted with the idea that was forming in her mind, she clapped both hands about Darvin's ears. When he looked up, stunned at the ringing in his head, she got up and, twisting one of his ears, said, 'Come along now, you naughty boy!' and led him to the bedroom.

Chance

Ord felt gutted. He read the letter again.

It informed him that he was no longer required to report for work. Although he had been trained as a Carer, most of his working life had been spent at the Hub. The Hub was his life. How, he wondered, could he cope with all the free time he had on his hands? Who was there to meet when all his mates were working? The first few days were a welcome rest, but now he was just kicking his heels.

He looked at the letter again: its plain print, its matter-of-factness, its brevity, its total lack of any sympathy or recognition of responsibility, the absence of any mention of the future and the illegible signature at the bottom made him slam it down on the table. He decided to go out for yet another walk.

He tramped the empty streets, reflecting on how much he had changed in the last few weeks. One good thing, he thought, was that he did not have the blinding headaches anymore. He couldn't think why they had stopped, although he was mighty glad they had. He wondered if it had anything to do with not having to stack boxes anymore. He also realized that he was no longer citing the slogans. It had gone quiet inside. He felt different. It was like he knew he had a past because he had memories, but somehow they did not seem to belong to him. They seemed to belong to someone else. He shook his head. He felt as if he had broken free of something, of an earlier self, or... He didn't know; just felt better, but empty. And when he slept, he was dreamless.

Looking up, he noticed that the sky was overcast and rain threatened. He turned his collar up and increased his pace to burn off the frustration he felt at having nothing to do. As he turned a street corner, he stopped in his tracks. It was that servicer – Eva.

She was seated on a pink bench looking at the palms of her hands. Ord hesitated. He wondered whether he should speak. The last thing he wanted to do was to burden her with his problems and he did not know if he could trust himself not to. But before he could decide, she had noticed him.

He stepped forward, his head bobbing up and down, and said, 'I thought it was you.' It occurred to him that she might have forgotten him. 'Do you remember me?' he asked awkwardly, remembering his non-performance.

'Yes,' she said and looked away as if he had intruded upon her thoughts.

Ord was on the point of leaving, feeling he was in the way, when she said, 'Did anything ever come of that C80? You know, you said you filled one in?'

Ord sat down. As he did so, the plastic bench sagged. He sat slightly apart from her, but stared into the same empty space as if this was all they could share.

'No. Nothing,' he answered after a while. 'That's why I'm here now, just wandering around, killing time.'

'No work?' Eva asked.

'Yeah. No more work.' He noticed her hair was turning black at the roots and that she was, as he'd thought, Asian. Without make-up, he noticed her smooth, wheat-coloured skin. As she seemed lost in thought, Ord thought it best to say nothing but no longer felt he was intruding.

Eva was wondering how much longer she could carry on doing what she was doing. She was wondering if she could ever come out the same as she went in. She tried to follow the advice of those around her. It's only a job, they said. It's good money. Don't think about it so much, it's just like any other job really. Bit like caring for adults. It's sex therapy, they said. But then they'd been trained as Sex Servicers; she hadn't. She'd been a Carer. She felt it was changing her, making her cold somewhere where once she'd been warm. She loved the darling faces of the children at the nursery. Now she was being told to go through the motions like a true servicer. But it was tearing her Carer heart apart. She felt scared. Some of the men were horrible. She felt she was being carried away on a dark tide.

After a while, she spoke: 'It's just that I been wondering whether to do the same. You know, fill one in.'

Ord looked across. He noticed she was tangling and untangling her fingers. 'I wish I could say it would help, but I got no answer. It's done me no good. But then, what do you want to tell them? Maybe they'll listen to you.'

'I want my job back, that's all.'

'At the nursery?'

'Yeah.'

'Do you want to walk some?' Ord asked, seeing her lips were trembling. 'It's getting kind of cold. I know a place does a good soup. If you feel, you know, like... eating.'

Eva looked at Ord. It was getting cold. She'd forgotten how long she'd been sitting there. The wind had turned chilly. Maybe a hot soup would be good. She remembered he'd been a Carer, too, once. Maybe he wasn't like all the others. She got up.

'All right,' she replied, hardly looking at him and so softly her voice was lost on the wind.

As they walked along the deserted streets, Ord talked about what he'd been doing, or rather not doing, ever since he had been laid off work. While he talked, Eva also felt she wanted to talk. To tell it all. To unburden. To tell the unwanted what she wanted. To tell him all about what was going on in her mad head, day in day out. But then she thought, better not, lest it turn into a muddle and he thought she was going individ. Who was he, anyway? For all she knew, he might be like all the rest. And wasn't that just it? Her feelings about men were changing. And was it any wonder, if all she ever did was suck off every stranger who came to the parlour? Old Joe would say, 'Oh, it's only servicing.' And then, 'But it's got to be good service,' wagging his finger in her face.

She looked up when Ord said all his workmates shunned him. She noticed how his light brown hair was greying and how deep the lines on his face were etched.

'I'm an outcast,' Ord continued, looking across at her. 'For all anyone cares, I may as well be Out there.'

Eva felt shocked. She was on the point of asking him what in the Codes he was thinking, but stopped. She knew if they did not want him at the Hub anymore and they still hadn't found work for him, he would be junked as soon as you could say Dovan the Great. She hoped they would find him a job.

'Do you think you're going individ?' she asked, averting her eyes as soon as she said it.

'I don't know. But something's changing. Inside me. I don't find answers in the slogans anymore. It's like I... have to make sense of everything. It's not easy. I feel empty, like I got nothing to think back to.' Ord stopped, not knowing what else to say.

Eva looked away. Poor sod, she thought and started to tell him about her life in the nursery. As they talked, the wind blew harder and they drew closer to better hear each another. They carried on till, turning a corner, a strong gust took them by surprise and they found themselves huddled together, bracing themselves against its blast. How and who had done it, Ord didn't have time to think, but somehow he thought he may have crooked his arm or Eva had put hers through his, but, whatever... he knew they were now walking arm in arm. Suddenly, he felt a wave of warmth course through his veins. He could hardly believe that such a simple act could have such an effect. It made him realize how lonely he had become. None of his workmates spoke to him anymore. It hurt. And now this touch meant so much more.

He stole a look at Eva. He wondered if there wasn't something special about her. Maybe there was something inside her trying to get out, too. 'She's beautiful,' he heard himself say and was immediately puzzled at the thought.

Soon they reached the tiny restaurant he liked to visit. They bundled in out of the cold wind. They ordered several small dishes and asked for the noodles to be brought last. As they ate, they talked.

'Where do you live, Eva?'

'You know the parlour? Well, the lane to the left goes around the back and there's a few huts there. Mine's a lean-to that's a faded blue.'

'Handy for work,' Ord said and could have bitten his tongue off there and then. Hurriedly, he carried on: 'It used to take me about forty minutes to get to the Hub. The walkways were always packed.'

'So where do you live?'

'District 5. You know it?'

'No.'

'That doesn't surprise me. There's only dormitories there.'

'What, no shopping precinct?'

'Nope. Nothing but dorms. That's why I used to stop off at your district, the Old Bio, and then walk on home.'

'What do you do now you're not working?'

'Walk a lot,' Ord replied, managing a laugh.

'Why don't you go and see some movies or something?'

'Well, I would but... I still get an allowance, you know. But I don't have as much money as I used to. I eat out a lot and read stuff, but when you're not working, you don't need to play. I don't go to the parlours anymore. Don't feel like it. Strange. When you work, you need to play. I dunno, it's all kinda back to front.'

Ord paused to look around. It seemed to him there were an odd bunch of customers there. One very fat man was squeezed behind a table making it, as well as the chair he sat on, seem disproportionately small. In the other corner was his exact opposite – a man as thin as a hatchet. The third customer was opening and shutting his mouth like a fish. Looking back at Eva, Ord saw her smile. She must have been thinking the same. What a perfect smile, he thought, as they chuckled behind the steam from the bowls of rice they had raised to their mouths.

In between great mouthfuls, Ord spluttered: 'Yeah, I used to meet me mates 'n have a drink and 'n stuff 'n it was good, s'pose. But now I don't. Everything feels different. Can't put a handle on it, but enough about me. What d'you do in your free time?'

'Well, I go shopping. I like shopping. Don't always buy things. Just like looking, picking at things. Go to the movies. Like sitting in the dark and getting lost in a good movie.' Ord smiled and pushed a small dish of boiled chicken toward her, gesturing her to take the last slice.

'Do you have anything you like to do?' Eva asked.

'Well, like I said, everything's changed so much. But I like watching...' Ord paused a moment, 'the sun rise and set.'

'Yeah?'

'It's the colours and the stillness I like.'

Eva carried on eating, watching him but betraying no sign of dismay or any great interest.

'I guess it sounds kind of crazy but it's beautiful.'

Eva thought of the first Carer slogan – Caring is Sharing – and wondered if Ord had already gone individ.

'I think,' Ord said, 'it's 'cos I find it hard to understand a lot of things that up to now I just... accepted. So now, I try to keep it simple. It's like I don't want my head full of questions.' He gave a shrug. 'A lot of things just don't mean the same anymore.'

'Like what?'

He paused. 'Well... like the slogans. They don't fit anymore.'

Eva stirred uneasily in her chair.

Just then two bowls of hot noodles were placed in front of them. As they slurped them up, Ord thought he'd better not talk too much about what he was going through. He wondered if he weren't going into overdrive trying to cope with cold stares and turned backs. Maybe he was that man, grasping at straws, hoping beyond hope, creating his own reality, till he could not tell which was real – mind or world.

But what he saw now, he thought, as he raised his eyes and saw Eva chewing on a slice of soft pork, were coral pink lips, alluring almond eyes and a woman who was not what he'd imagined. He wanted to put out his hand to pull back the long half-blonde black hair that covered one side of her face. Not daring to, he smiled shyly and looked back into the steam rising from his soup.

Eva felt better. Maybe it was the walk, maybe the soup... no definitely the soup, she thought. And, looking across at Ord's pale face, she thought, maybe I've found a friend, even if he is odd. And Codes, do I need a friend! Looking past him, she noticed the time. 'Is that the time?' she asked. 'I'm going to have to hurry.'

Ord looked at the steamed-up face of the digital clock. It was coming up to five. They finished off their noodles, split the bill, and parted outside the tiny eating place.

Ord returned home, feeling as if he was walking on air. It seemed to him the best thing that had happened to him for a long time. If what he was seeing was true, he warned himself. Before she had headed back to work, (poor Eva, he thought, remembering how her face had dropped) he had stood awkwardly and she had put out her hand and touched him lightly, just like she had done that time at the parlour. It's the small things, he thought, that show the feelings. 'Friends,' she'd said. And he had smiled. He wondered how long it would be before they met again. He wanted to know more about her.

A Meeting of Minds

Gorvik strode along the Topround corridor. He was thinking about his love-hate relationship with politics. It made him grit his teeth. On the one hand, he would rather spend his time in the laboratory with co-researchers. That was what he found most satisfying. On the other hand, he knew if he did not fight their corner on various committees, particularly the influential Home Affairs Committee, they would not have enough money to do any research.

His counterparts on the committees – he doubted if he could call them colleagues – were either consummate politicians who never committed themselves to any policy for fear of not being able to pull out if it went wrong or civil servants who defended the status quo because they did not want to create more work. Don't rock the boat, leave the forms as they are was their motto.

It riled him to think how conservative the majority were. The nobles – Darvin, Q'zar, Valchek and O – were always harking back to what they imagined to be a golden age. Darvin was only interested in holding onto power. He knew he could rely on Lara as well as the nobles to block any challenge on controversial issues. He would arrange the agenda for meetings so that thorny issues were forced into the limited time allotted to 'any other business.' If he was not sure of support, a backroom deal was the solution. In short, he opposed reform.

Although Q'zar ran his department very efficiently, his was a narrow, elitist view. Valchek epitomised the 'front-man' – he could talk about anything and everything as if he cared. But he was a turncoat. His allegiance depended upon how much he could gain. As for O, he and his department may as well not exist. True, he did carry a vote, but since he never came to any meetings he could be discounted. Of the other three, citizens who, like himself, had reached the top through dint of talent and hard work, Arron was the archetypal civil servant. He was an admirable person – principled and intelligent. But, alas, another defender of the status quo. Small changes, yes, but anything radical, no. Lara was Darvin's rubber stamp. But Sovran, she was different. Thanks to her leadership, Media's use of technology was nothing less than brilliant.

At the last meeting, Gorvik had detected a willingness on her part to at least listen to his argument. It was for this reason he'd asked his secretary to arrange a private meeting. Her motivation might be different, more emotional possibly, but never mind that, he thought. If they could reach an agreement, it could prove extremely useful since only she had the means to address citizens directly. He had a gut feeling that the committee room was no longer the correct forum for change. He had to get Media on his side. Let the people have it, let them discuss it, let them judge for or against. If we can't change the Seventh top down, we'll do it bottom up, he thought as the door to Sovran's apartment came into view.

***

Sovran glanced at the time. She was thinking a man as busy as Gorvik would not request a meeting to chat over a drink. He obviously wanted to harness her support on the free clone issue. She would listen. But, at bottom, she did not feel very sympathetic. There was one thing they had in common, however. In the same way, he could not get committee members to discuss that issue, she couldn't get them to face up to the question of expanding Outward.

Code knows, she thought, here we are, cooped up in a densely populated city, unable to even talk about these issues. Dare she challenge that taboo, she wondered? She felt she would have to one day, but when? It was a huge risk. She would be putting her job on the line. According to Security, Media's job was to communicate the rights of tradition, not the values of an uncertain future.

This made her think of the man who enforced those rules – Q'zar. At lower level committees, their secretaries met frequently to discuss how to present the news. They selected what should be shown, then discussed in nit-picking detail how to depict each event. What slant should be put upon it, what subliminal messages should be inserted and how. There were even times when events were staged to create the news.

She remembered the Pharo Affair. She had been a young journalist then and she was over the moon to be put on that story. It made her. It was the break she'd waited for and she rode it for all it was worth. She also remembered it was the first time she'd met Q'zar. Her first impression had not changed one iota. He was a control freak. The policy of nipping trouble in the bud that he'd proposed and gained permission to pilot had now become accepted practice. It was hailed as the major factor behind the fall in the crime rate. But it led to arrests being made prior to the crime. Once an arrest was made, there was no recourse to justice. There was no judicial procedure.

The whole society was geared to consensus, and, as the proverb had it, the nail that stuck up was hammered down.

The official role of Media was to distract public attention from the realization that they were the last civilization by creating an illusion of well-being – 'substitute reality' was the term. But the result of so many years of careful manipulation was that few citizens realized or even cared about the distortions anymore. Life was so comfortable it sedated thought. All the talk was about cooking, new products, who was on the Big Show, who would win the championship, fashion, gossip, anything, except the fact that stared them in the face: they were the last outpost of humankind.

Sovran got up and walked across to a long window that ran the length of one side of her penthouse suite. She looked down at the tubular walkways that coiled away from the base of the Tower between high-rise buildings. Then, raising her head, she gazed out over the forest at the faint contour of mountain ranges in the distance. The dread that citizens have of the Outside, it has to change she thought. We can't carry on pretending. We have to face our fears one day. I need an ally. I'll listen to him.

The door chime startled her. She walked briskly toward the door. As she approached it, she could see from the screen above that it was Gorvik. She opened the door.

'Hello, right on time,' she said with a smile and waved him in.

'Ever punctual, you know.' He smiled back, noticing she was wearing ivory white slacks and a loose-fitting blouse.

Once Gorvik had settled himself on a long beige sofa, she asked, 'Would you like something to drink?'

'Thank you. Tea would be fine.'

She did not need to make the tea. Chuck – the name she had given her home automation system – began the process in the kitchen. After exchanging a few pleasantries, Sovran fetched it when Chuck called.

After taking a few sips, Gorvik leaned forward and said, 'I'm a busy person, Sovran, and I know you are. So, if you don't mind, I'll come straight to the point.'

'Go ahead.'

'The reason I wanted to see you is to talk about the issue of free cloning. As you know, every time I bring it up at meetings it has failed. Darvin is implacably opposed to it as are the others. But, correct me if I'm wrong, I thought I detected an interest from you. What you said about resurrection cloning was a fair point, though – I do apologize – at the time I thought it a side issue. To be honest, at that point I'd reached the end of my tether,' Gorvik said, shaking his head.

'Hardly surprising,' said Sovran. 'There's enough deadwood on that committee to make anybody who's got any get-up-and-go scream.'

Gorvik chuckled. 'Couldn't agree more.' But then, looking at Sovran more seriously, he added, 'It is odd, though. Don't you think? Usually advances in science and technology make societies more liberal. And yet, Joypolis seems the exception. It's so conservative.' He paused to tug the end of his beard. 'If that Seventh were amended, resurrection cloning would be available, you know.'

'I guess it would, but it's not the real reason you want the Seventh changed, is it?'

'True.'

'So what is?'

'Well, as I said at the last meeting, I don't like the present system of conditioning clones to do specific tasks.

Machines could do that kind of work. That tea you just fetched, it could have been brought in by a simple robot. In fact, you probably know, the reason why machines aren't used – and you'll have to excuse this heresy...'

Sovran laughed. 'Oooh, I love heresies. Let's hear it.

'Well, you can call it a historical accident, but after the Andradist Uprising, all research into artificial intelligence came to a halt. Koron advocated a mechanized society in which robots, not clones, would lead the struggle for survival. Well, whatever Koron said or did certainly put a lot of people off robots. The effects can be seen now in the way we are surrounded by LPRs. I want to see people cloned for intelligence. Let machines do the repetitive jobs these Low Personal Responders do.'

'Hmm. Clones from real people.'

'I'll be frank, I need your help. I can't make any headway on this issue at committee level. I'm banging my head against a brick wall. Sovran, you and I of all people know how Darvin got to be Chairman.'

Gorvik was referring to the way he and Sovran had agreed to withdraw their candidacy to avoid a split on the Home Affairs Committee. They agreed that situation must be avoided. The lessons of the past, particularly the Andradist Uprising, had not been forgotten. It was in this way that Darvin, the rank outsider, became Chairman.

'Yes,' Sovran replied, thinking back to that time. 'Looking back, it's a huge irony.'

Gorvik nodded with a heartfelt sigh of regret.

'But tell me,' Sovran began, 'with real clones, would they still die young? And be less human? Unable to have children. And what about Lara's point?'

'No, they wouldn't be less human or die early. The ones we have now die young for two reasons. One is sequential cloning, and...'

'Come again?'

'The vast majority are cloned from clones who have also been cloned from clones...'

'Got you.'

'They're all duplets.'

'And the second reason?'

'The indoctrination. It takes... I'm not sure how to put this, but in plain language, it takes the spark out of them. They are not exposed to the higher ideals that make us special – ideals that inspire some to devote their whole life to a cause or even sacrifice their life for the greater good. They have needs, but not love. By setting the range of possible experience, chemical-semiosis prevents them from being fully human. Of course, the coding unravels, and, though the time frame is not hard and fast, it takes the form of a natural decline into senility. And then, as you know, our laws permit a merciful death. The older models deconstruct when they get somewhere between thirty-five to forty years old, the newer ones around ten years later.'

'Not very nice, wouldn't you say? Manufactured, indoctrinated, dying young, childless and no love?'

'Yes.'

'And how's all this done?'

'Well, computers are used to stimulate reward or punishment to a variety of images and signals. For example, an image of a clone touching a female citizen results in a shock.'

'But what about the Carers? Surely, they're conditioned to care?'

'True. Dovan recognized a contradiction there and recommended what he termed 'mundane measures' to stop caring overflowing into a loving relationship.'

'And what exactly did he mean by that?'

'Well, if it is known that two Carers are meeting and forming a relationship, Security sees to it that their work shifts are altered so they find it impossible to meet. You can't get much more mundane than that, can you?' Gorvik chuckled.

Sovran found nothing to laugh about. 'Don't you think there's a moral issue here?'

'Yes, of course.' Gorvik coughed before continuing: 'They faced extinction. Dovan and his followers chose bio-semiosis because they believed it was the only way to guarantee survival. The moral issues must have seemed insignificant in comparison to the greater good. They got the social stability they were after alright. You could say they were too successful. It has stifled progress in other areas. Artificial intelligence is one of them. We need to do a lot more research on AI but can't because of a stubborn resistance to change. Citizens seem to think the same. Don't you agree? They can think some things, but not other things.'

'It may surprise you, but I do,' Sovran said, looking straight back into his eyes. 'I feel locked in, unable to discuss numerous issues, and, whoops, my turn for a heresy, especially the question of expanding Outward. We can't even talk about it.'

Throwing her hands up, she stood up and walked over to the window. She didn't like Gorvik's cold, scientific manner of thinking. We're not on the same wavelength, she thought.

'The two issues are related, you know,' Gorvik said, wondering if he'd said something wrong.

'Yes, I think so too.'

'The LPRs provide the economic stability that prevents the shocks that force change – such as the need to expand Outward. And the other issue which I tried to alert the committee to is the gradual decline in the birth rate. I can't help but think that the fact that the clones comprise the bulk of the workforce has something to do with it. You see, it provides one of the mainstays for survival – production of food. When a society becomes this artificial, surely it starts to break free from laws of natural selection?'

Sovran said nothing, but it occurred to her that the cause might be far simpler. If you weren't too fussy, the Aesthetics School were offering sexual partners at very reasonable prices. The sheer convenience of the service must, she thought, lessen the desire for steady sex-love relationships.

After a pause, Gorvik continued, 'It'll be a major problem in two generations' time. Look at how more and more births are arranged via IVF. A fresh approach to cloning is one way to re-ignite the impetus for change, such as expanding Out.'

'But it's worse than that, isn't it? Three quarters of the population are clones. We're surrounded by them and yet we don't know or care about them. We don't know who they're related to. I can't tell my readers we're using humans, rearing them to be docile slaves and discarding them when they deconstruct. They've accepted the situation for so long, they think it's normal. They believe the clones are sub-human and don't matter.' Sovran shook her head. 'Media, me, we've fed them that line for so long it has given substance to the prejudice. It's sickening.'

After a long pause, Sovran continued: 'You walk around the city. You see how the people accept the apartheid as normal – separate work areas, separate living areas, separate walkways, sports clubs, restaurants, bars, sex parlours, everything.'

'Sovran, it's got to change. If we can't change this at committee level, then it's got to come from the people. Only you have the means to reach them.'

'I could use resurrection cloning as an angle. It's emotional, but that's where its appeal lies. It might get people thinking about the Seventh. I could then lead them into questioning why we can't change anything just because it's constitutional. It might prise the debate open on the clone issue as well as attitudes toward the Outside. But I'm being too optimistic. Nobody thinks about politics anymore. They want everything to be decided for them.'

'Do it. I'm prepared to submit an article in support and put my name to it: 'Real Clones from Real People'.'

'Hey! That's a good line. If you lose your job, we'll take you on!' Sovran said, jokingly.

Gorvik chortled.

'Let me have it,' said Sovran more sombrely. 'I'm not making any promises. I've got Q'zar breathing down my neck. But you never know. If the right moment presents itself and a bombshell is needed...'

'You'll stick it under his ass?' asked Gorvik, not disappointed to see Sovran crack up laughing. Glancing at his watch, he thought this might be the right moment to leave. 'Well, I better go, but I hope the image of Q'zar blown to pieces keeps you in good spirits.'

'It's been an interesting talk. Let's keep in touch on this one,' said Sovran, walking to the door with him.

'Yes, it has. Thank you, Sovran.' Gorvik turned and shook her hand lightly.

As he walked away from her apartment, he was pleased. Good woman, he thought. Feisty. Tired of this walled-in mentality. Although he had not got a clear commitment, he felt there had been a meeting of minds. But there was one thing he dared not mention – he had already started free cloning.

This was a secret known only to himself and two of his most trusted colleagues. So frustrated had he been at Darvin taking the chairmanship, he had decided to go it alone. He had cloned three individuals, one from his DNA and the others from two colleagues'. The papers submitted to the authorities made it appear as if four or five separate experiments were being conducted. This had shielded them from suspicion. But the clones would soon be fourteen years old and would surely begin to ask why they were being treated differently. The moment their existence came to the notice of the authorities, there would be hell to pay. Where were their papers? Who were they? The parents? The donors? Free clones!

This was the bombshell that was forcing Gorvik's hand and he wanted the storm to break from another quarter so he could present his three protégés as proof of the success of free cloning and so clinch the argument for the reform of the Clone Laws.

The Outside

As weeks turned into months, Ord had no idea what to do with all the free time he had on his hands. He had given up trying to talk to his co-workers. They shunned him to a man. He had walked every street in Joypolis and played away his last allowance at the game centres.

He sat in the silence of his room thinking about Krm. What did he mean when he claimed ideas had been put in our heads? Every time Ord thought about this, it led him to the relation of citizen to clone. This, in turn, always led to the image of parenthood. And when he tried to frame a question about the nature of that parenthood, his mind went blank.

He would then think of Eva. Meeting her helped. Even though their meetings were brief, it was the only thing he looked forward to. It was strange, he thought, how they were slowly getting to know each another in a way that he'd never experienced before. He realized his earlier view of her was completely wrong. Distorted. And it was an attitude shared by all the Packers he knew. Could that be a coincidence, he wondered? Or had that, as Krm said, also been created? He ran his fingers through his hair and struggled to think it through, but again his mind went blank.

Getting up from the sofa, he walked over to the window. He stood there watching the tops of trees swaying in the distance. On the spur of the moment, he thought, 'I'll go there.' He turned, took his jerkin from where it hung behind the door and pulled it on as he opened the door. 'Anything's better than being cooped up like this all day. Out there, that's where I'll go,' he urged himself as he checked he had locked the door.

He jogged down the stairs, telling himself there was nothing more to lose. Nothing made sense anymore. No work, no friends, just time, time, time. All this time on my hands. I try to think, I go blank. Just nothing. Empty. Feeling his throat constrict, he kicked out at a bin at the bottom of the stairs and ran off as it rolled off clattering.

When he came to a deserted street, he slowed his pace to a walk. He shaded his eyes from the sun's glare. Thinking of the sun, he remembered how he had watched it that morning. Sole friend, he thought now sweating beneath its blaze. Give me strength, he implored. Help me know who and what I am and why no one cares. He stopped and, squatting on his haunches, pulled his head down into his own shadow.

When he felt calmer, he got up and continued walking. He knew he must be close to the city's boundary. Reaching a junction, he saw the road to his left did in fact lead to the perimeter. He could see security posts on either side of the road at regular intervals with cameras perched on top. Hearing a humming sound, he swung round. Seeing it was only an unmanned garbage vehicle, he relaxed. He watched it pass and move slowly up the road he faced. It left a sickly smell in its wake that made him cover his nose. He turned away from the stale stink and walked toward the perimeter.

Ord noticed how silent it was. A million people were huddled at the centre and yet, here, there was scarcely a sound. No buildings. Just rubbish tips on either side of the road. Dead ends.

When he reached the end of the road, he looked down at the lumpiness of the earth where the tarmac ended. Turning, he looked back and realized he had never seen the Tower from so far away. He looked back at the trees. They too seemed different, now he was closer. Gulping, he stepped off the edge. Dry clods of earth crumpled beneath his shoes. He took a few steps, then more, until the trees began to loom closer. He could feel his heart beating, but reminded himself of the alternative – boxed up in his room.

When the ground grew rougher, he found himself almost stumbling toward the trees. When he reached them, he wondered if he should circle the city or go deeper among the trees. He was not worried about getting lost: he had his locator on his wrist. A sensor activated it whenever he left his room and flashed a silver arrow in the direction of his room. He decided to go deeper.

He continued walking, feeling both excited and afraid. Occasionally, he paused to look at the bushes. Some were in flower. He smelt their fragrance and watched the insects that hovered over them. He noticed some insects crawling into the flowers. The sweet smell was unlike any he had smelt before. He touched one of the flowers. Withdrawing his hand, he noticed a fine film of yellow dust on his fingers. It did not burn. Even so, he wiped it off on his trousers and walked on, looking from side to side.

The forest was not as dense as he imagined. In some places the trees were spaced far apart, but when he looked up, he noticed how their branches reached out and touched those of neighbouring trees. He looked at their dark streaked trunks and ran his fingers up and down them to feel their texture.

At length, he came to a small stream. He had of course seen water before, but never coursing naturally. He stepped down the slope and squatted beside the stream. Watching its gurgling headlong rush, he thought it almost playful. Although he was still unsure of everything around him, he was beginning to relax and enjoy these new sensations. He did not feel threatened. In fact, quite the opposite: he felt elated. He broke a blade of grass and placed it on the water and watched it lose itself in flashes of silver light.

It was unlike anything he had seen before. Very different to the virtual images of the game centres and the plastic shrubbery of the parks, he thought. Spellbound, he continued to watch. When he lay back to rest, he noticed the sunlight filtering through the trees. Sitting up, he looked at how the patterning of shade around him shifted with the wind. He smiled. It was as if the forest was breathing. He liked it. After resting, he got up and walked along the stream. He recalled a random find on his home computer and wondered if this was the kind of thing shepherds did.

Crossing the stream, he walked up the gentle slope of its bank. Reaching the top, he saw a mound at the bottom of a treeless glade of tall grass. Suddenly a shrill cry made him duck. Crouched, he caught sight of a brightly coloured bird darting into a tree. Glancing at his locator, he realized he'd been gone much longer than he'd thought. Before heading back, he keyed in the coordinates it showed on its screen. He decided he would come here again and investigate that mound.

THE WATCHERS

The Watchers was the term used to refer to Joypolis' police force. It was apt since most of their work involved observation through closed-circuit television or eavesdropping with recording devices. The Security Department justified the presence of so many hidden eyes and ears by pointing out that it was grossly undermanned. What Q'zar did not realize, although at times he suspected it, was that this chronic shortage of personnel was not caused by a lack of funds or the alleged priority of other projects, but policy. There were a number of influential people, among whom Darvin was one, who had no wish to see a large security force – they had a tendency to become small armies and grow impatient with the slow decision-making processes of government. In short, Darvin had no wish to see Q'zar, or anyone else, at the head of a modern Praetorian Guard.

Q'zar sat in a long, windowless room listening to one of his officers give an account of a video recording of Ord's movements.

'Of course we don't know what happened after he crossed the perimeter, but we can see him walking in a straight line right up to the forest. Once he enters, we lose sight of him.' Stopping the recording, the Watchman said,

'Given the time he was away, we can assume he went deep into the forest.'

'Um,' was all Q'zar said.

'What should we do, Domo?' Domo was a term used by lower ranks to their superiors.

'Do?'

'I'm concerned. The clone might have picked up some disease. And even...'

Q'zar could sense anxiety in his quavering voice. Although he could easily have dispelled his fears, he allowed him to continue more for sport than any other reason.

'...contaminate others. We know the Outside is polluted. Everyone who came from there died of radioactive sickness. Children were deformed from birth...'

'Yes,' said Q'zar baldly. 'It's true. But that was a long time ago. And the forest, bar that grey area we know nothing about, seems to be renewing itself. The number of birds has also increased recently. That may be significant. Look for patterns, do you understand? Patterns.

'Now, I don't want you to stop this soon-to-be-junked clone from going to the Outside.' Q'zar raised a hand to silence the protest that was forming in the Watchman's eyes. 'I know we can't follow him, but we may learn something about the Outside without exposing ourselves to danger. Observe his behaviour when he gets back. Did he look ill? If so, have him report for a medical. If not, we'll assume he's all right. Have a new sensor installed in his room so we can read the coordinates on his locator. That way we'll know exactly where he went. Is that clear?'

'Yes, Domo,' replied the Watcher, his eyes shining with admiration.

'And not a word of this to anyone, do you understand?' Q'zar looked piercingly at each Watcher in turn.

'Yes, Domo!' the three shouted in unison.

Warton's eyes narrowed as soon as Q'zar left the room. Zuriko will pay a packet for this, he thought. A clone venturing to the Outside without permission! Returning with the risk of disease! Sanctioned by none other than Q'zar himself! He rubbed his hands together as he wondered which sex friend he would choose as payment. But, he warned himself, be careful. On this occasion, unlike previous ones, only three of them had been present. If he was caught, the old man, as he liked to call Q'zar, would come down on him like a ton of bricks. He would need to cover his ass. It would have to be planned. Zuriko would think of something, he thought.

'Wonder what's got the old man so rattled?' he asked nonchalantly.

'It's the Outside,' replied Chu, the lieutenant who had been explaining Ord's movements. 'He hates it and everything to do with it.'

'What, even more than we do?' said Warton.

'If you enjoyed the lifestyle of a noble, you'd be exactly the same,' replied the third Watchman, a man called Hersh. 'The Outside is the opposite of everything they admire – art, culture, beauty.'

'Well, we'd better keep this one under wraps,' Warton retorted. As he moved off to his desk, he was thinking a fat lot Hersh knows about the life of nobles. All they care about is money so they can buy art, culture, beauty and whatever else they want.

Ironically, the speed at which Warton had risen through the ranks of Watchers had not dispelled his discontent. Quite the opposite, it had fuelled it. He thought it sprang from boredom or something that was so deep he could never hope to fathom it. He blamed it on living in such a confined city. Sometimes, he wished something would come from the Outside. Might liven things up, he thought as he reached down, pulled open a drawer and took out a tube of *Helpups*. Flipping the top open, he tipped one out. After admiring its minty whiteness, he popped it into his mouth. Sucking on it, he smiled when he recalled the commercial: *Helpups are unputdownable!*

Leaning back till his chair rested against the wall, he stared up at the ceiling. Yes, he thought, this chip's worth bargaining over. As a horizon of intrigue opened before his mind's eye, he realized how much he enjoyed scheming. It gave spice to his life. Even the betrayal of Q'zar's trust was fun, he thought. But beware, he told himself. He knew he was getting more and more enmeshed in Zuriko's web of deceit. She was far more dangerous than Q'zar. He was predictable. She was not. Cunning bitch, he thought as his chair came banging down to face the paperwork on his desk.

***

After Q'zar left the room, he took an elevator to the Watchtower. Stepping out onto its observatory platform, he gazed out over the forest. Yes, he thought, it is renewing itself. Should they dare send a patrol out?

Looking south, he saw the grey area that started as a thin strip before broadening and running for the entire length of what appeared to be a valley. For some reason, the trees there remained grey throughout the year. He believed it was a blighted area that had not recovered from the precipitation of chemical poisons. To the north and east were mountain ranges. Some were volcanic and occasionally erupted.

The thought of the Outside made him feel uneasy. He began to walk slowly around the parapet with his hands clasped behind him. After the first wave of travellers, only savages and mutants had ever come out of the forest. But that was long ago and no one had come in his or his father's lifetime. No, he concluded, there are no barbarians at the gate. But within the gates...

He stopped, gripped the rail and peered down at the city. As he surveyed Joypolis, he felt an immense pride. Yet a nagging doubt niggled at him. The greatest threat to security so far, he thought, has always come from internal disputes among the Directorate. He recalled Gorvik's demands for reforms of the Clone Laws. And, now, Sovran was moving toward endorsing his position because she seemed to think free cloning would lead to the demise of the laws that separated clone from citizen. Gorvik had not made his position clear on that issue. But even so, he thought, they're playing with fire. He thought of Darvin's weak leadership. All he ever thought about was Zuriko. He was her lap dog, divulging official secrets. He shook his head in disbelief at the power she and her sex stars wielded. How they exploited their sex for power and how so many men, especially the weak but also the strong made weak, succumbed. Media's to blame he thought. Makes idols of them. But his lips curled with even greater contempt when he thought of Valchek. He suspected he'd had sex with a clone. The babbling of a deconstructing clone was not sufficient evidence, but Q'zar was unable to rid himself of the suspicion. The law was clear: no sexual relations between clone and citizen. This applied to nobles as well as citizens. The splendour of Joypolis dulled momentarily as he weighed the possibility that beneath its glittering façade lay a rotten core.

This, he concluded, is the price we pay for peace. He felt more and more that the events he was witnessing pointed to one thing and one thing alone: decadence. Taking a last look at the Greylands, he thought it is well that there is nothing Out there. Because if there were, Joypolis would crumble at the slightest threat. We have no defence.

None. We must learn more about the Outside – even if it is from a worthless clone. Without information, we are helpless. This last word made him spin on his heels and exit the Watchtower.

A Word

Inwardly, Ord sensed it was over. There was no going back to the Hub or anything else that had once seemed normal. He decided to cross the perimeter again. This would be the fifth time. True, he had hesitated to go back. He felt guilty. If he didn't go back, he thought they might ask him to come back to work. But when he'd been told to remain within certain districts, he knew it would only be a matter of time before they came and took him to the Encrypt.

As he slipped his jerkin on, he supposed the Watchers must know. Maybe they'd be waiting this time. But he could not stay in his room all day. It was torture. He'd called Eva countless times, but she wasn't answering. He had a rough idea why. Last time they met he had told her what he had seen on the Outside. It scared her.

It all seemed so clear now. Wasn't it always like that? Understanding too late. Eva was tired that day, dog-tired. A child could have seen that. Her eyes had no sparkle... but she had come through the rain to meet him. They were downcast... but they'd looked up at him appealingly. And what had he done? Yap. He couldn't hold it in – what he'd done, what he'd seen, where he'd been, it was all so important and she'd listened, given him her Carer heart until she could bear it no longer. She'd got up, made some excuse and left, leaving him with all his words dangling. So many words, he thought bitterly, and none worth a single act of kindness. She had come to ask something. Why couldn't he have realized it? Why couldn't he have seen that she needed him to listen, that the world did not revolve around him, that her world was as real, important, and as punishingly harsh as his. 'Fool, fool,' he said, slamming the door.

He glanced at his locator. The Watchers must know, he told himself. So why hadn't they come? He looked up and down the corridor. It was quiet. The thought that one day they will come made him quicken his step.

***

An hour or so later, he was walking the same path through the forest. Once again, he felt the same sense of wonder. Just to see how the light filtered through the trees creating a patchwork of shifting shades at his feet lightened his spirits. In Joypolis, all colours were primary and most shapes uniform. Today, the boughs were creaking in the wind and the leaves shaken so hard they roared. How different it all is, he thought. Most Joypolitan sounds were electronic – beeps and bleeps, the humming of one machine to another. There was music, almost everywhere you went, but something he had noticed recently was how often there was more than one tune being piped in the background. The result was noise. But here, all sounds were living. Natural, he supposed, was the word for it.

He walked on, puzzling over why Joypolitans had never ventured out. Perhaps they were wrong: perhaps the Outside was not the forbidding place they had been led to believe. He felt his head twinge, as if a light had fused inside. Looking around, not only did it seem safe, but it looked like a garden of unparalleled beauty. Thinking such thoughts, it suddenly struck him how much he had changed. Here he was thinking thoughts that a year ago would have been unthinkable. He looked back to see if he could see the Tower. At first, he couldn't, but then he spotted its pinnacle appearing and disappearing like a trick of light. He realized there could be no real going back. Not now. Not as Ord the Packer.

He walked on, saddened and yet consoled. He wondered where these new thoughts came from. They were not from the slogans. If he continued to change at this rate, he wondered what he would be like in, say, another year. He had no idea and wandered on feeling lights popping in his head.

When he reached the small brook, he decided not to follow it but to cross straightaway. He climbed the opposite bank and saw the same mound with the solitary tree beside it beyond an open stretch of tall, waving grass. He wondered why he felt apprehensive about crossing the space. Reassuring himself that there was nothing to fear, he began to walk toward the mound.

The grass reached up to his waist and it took a few minutes to reach the spot. Even as he approached, he realized it had once been a building. When the grass gave way to ferns, he became aware of rubble beneath his feet. Getting down, he could see slabs that had once had a regular shape. When he reached the edge of the pile, he pulled the ferns aside to see what was beneath. It did not look to be much, but here and there he noticed shards of rusted iron. He walked around till he reached what must have formed the entrance. He could see why this part still stood – it was solid iron embedded in a concrete base. The doors had long since rotted and the solitary tree that stood nearby seemed to stand guard over the humped remains. He went over to it.

Seeing marks on the bark, he examined them. They looked as if they had been gouged out. He followed their shapes with his finger, believing they were symbols. He thought there were four. They were unlike any writing he'd ever seen. But he read them as he would pronounce the most similar in Joypolis' script. 'Bora'. It must be a name, he thought.

He ran his hand over the surface of the tree but, unable to discover any more clear markings, he stepped over its large roots to get to the other side. As he did so, he looked up and stopped in his tracks. There was a carving of a face. Stepping back from the tree, he viewed it head on. It was carved on a bulge. Ord stepped closer and admired the life-like image. The eyes seemed to stare out of the tree. He raised his hand to touch it. He felt the low bridge of the nose, the wide spread of lips and the grooves of teeth. He wondered if it had moved upward as the tree had grown. If it had not moved, then the person who had carved it must have worked from a platform. Strangely beautiful, he thought.

After a while, he went back to the mound and began to forage around, trying to see if he could find anything of interest. He fairly jumped out of his skin when his locator beeped. Time had flown by. He could hardly believe he had spent so much time in this place. It was time to go. He did not want to spend the night out here. Yet, as he walked back, for the first time, he didn't feel like going back.

Any Other Business

'Is there any other business?' Darvin asked as they approached the end of a meeting of the Home Affairs Committee.

Both Valchek and Q'zar raised their hands simultaneously and, although both deferred to one another, Darvin indicated Q'zar to speak first.

In a matter-of-fact tone, Q'zar began: 'I should like to inform the committee that the clone who was reported as deconstructing will soon be taken to the Encrypt to be euthanized. I mention this only as a formality to set the usual procedure in motion.'

Unexpectedly, Gorvik spoke up. 'I suppose you're referring to the one who was transferred out of the job he was trained for? Caused a rumpus at the Hub?'

'That's right,' Q'zar answered, wondering why Gorvik was bothering to state the obvious.

'What state is he in now?' asked Gorvik.

Q'zar replied, 'Oh, he's approaching the final stages.' And added, 'He may be questioned.' He was thinking if Ord had anything interesting to say about the Outside he would bring it up at a different meeting.

'What's the point of questioning him?' asked Darvin as he tidied some papers. 'We don't usually bother them with questions, do we?'

'Sometimes we do,' replied Q'zar, beginning to feel apprehensive. He had not told them that Ord had been to the Outside. He wanted to wait until he had questioned him to find out if it would be useful to send a patrol out on a fact-finding mission.

'Do you want to question him about that sign? The one he described in his C80,' asked Valchek.

'Yes, and other matters possibly.'

'Other matters?' asked Sovran, looking at Q'zar in a querulous fashion. 'What other matters?'

They know, thought Q'zar. His grey eyes took on a steely hue as he drew a deep breath and coldly enunciated the words, 'It came to our notice that he had crossed to the Outside. That's why we need to question him.'

Q'zar witnessed a visible, as well as an audible reaction, around the table. Valchek's jaw dropped. Sovran feigned equal astonishment by drawing her head back. Lara nervously covered her mouth. Sensing it was orchestrated, Q'zar continued: 'I think it might be to our advantage to question him as to what he did and saw Out there.'

'Ahem.' Valchek cleared his throat to signal his intention to speak. 'I don't want to seem, eh, impertinent, but did you *know* he was going to go beyond the perimeter, that is to say, were you *aware*...'

'No, no, of course not,' Q'zar lied, glaring into Valchek's bobbing face.

'Didn't know?' said Darvin, puffing himself up like a blowfish.

'There have been more sightings recently,' replied Q'zar, not doubting for a second that he was wasting his breath. 'In fact, a significant increase. We need information on what is going on Out there. And as none of us would dream of going beyond the limits of our jewelled city, it seemed a perfect opportunity – a clone, soon to be junked, could do the dirty work for us. We didn't know he'd crossed until later, of course. But after we found out, it struck me it might be useful to check how far he'd gone by checking his locator.'

'Sightings? Of what, may I ask?' asked the Chairman, relishing the pickle that Q'zar had got himself into.

'Animals, birds,' replied Q'zar. 'We need to know what it all means. Is the Outside beginning to regenerate? Why is one vast area grey?' he asked.

'Birds?' said Lara derisively. 'Be that as it may, shouldn't the matter have been discussed? At council or committee level? There are procedures, protocol, don't you know,' she said, beginning to raise her voice.

Q'zar remained silent, deciding it was futile to say anymore. To reply would have made it appear that he did, in fact, have something to answer for.

Valchek took up the baton. 'I agree. Protocol should have been adhered to. The Outside poses many dangers. Not least of which is disease. It is not a light matter. In fact, it's very serious and, frankly, I'm shocked.'

Seething inwardly, Q'zar swore he would nail Valchek one day.

Darvin decided it was time to step into the fray. He leaned forward and said, 'It would appear that this time, you really have overstepped the mark.' He glanced round the table; everyone present, even those who had not spoken, were nodding their heads. 'Procedures are there for very good reasons. Was he contaminated?'

'No.'

'Well, on this occasion, I'm inclined to overlook your misdemeanour, although I hasten to add that I consider it a serious breach of protocol.

'I doubt if the clone has anything to tell us of the...' Darvin waved a dismissive hand in the direction of the perimeter, 'but if you think it's useful then I have a suggestion. Given the fact that the clone has already reached a fragile mental state, a full-blown interrogation might prove too much. You know, the push that sends him over the edge. No, I think a subtler approach is required.'

Q'zar sat impassively as Darvin began to outline his proposal. He knew there was nothing he could do but accept whatever hare-brained scheme he had hatched. Even though Darvin was acting as if the idea had just occurred to him, Q'zar knew it was one favour traded for another,

'We'll get someone to tease his secrets out. That way we might avoid a total breakdown and loss of information.'

'And who have you in mind, Chairman?' asked Q'zar.

'No one, at this point. But let me consult with the head of the Aesthetics School. I seem to recall her saying something at a steering meeting not so long ago that there was someone who showed great expertise in this area. Can I take it that this alternative plan is accepted?' Darvin looked around with the satisfied air of someone who had stopped a full-scale dispute.

The next matter had to do with preparations for the banquet and ball. This event marked the high point of Joypolis' social calendar. It commemorated the founding of the city by staging an enactment of its history. The matters brought up were mostly of a financial nature – how much had been set aside, number of guests, the order of ceremonies, the entertainment, whether any changes should be made to last year's arrangements which were a huge success, and so on.

Q'zar sat through it with gritted teeth, scarcely listening. He wanted to know which of his three lieutenants had betrayed him. Suddenly, he became aware that Valchek was stating that a clone called Url had put forward the idea for changing the sorting method at the Hub. Before he could raise a question, Lara had brought up a separate item of business. This meant he had lost his opportunity. Feeling utterly defeated, he swore he would find the mole and put him behind bars.

LAIA

This was not an assignment Laia had requested. In fact, the more she thought about it, the more she wondered why she had given in to Zuriko. If only she had asked for time to think about it. Foolishly, it seemed now, she had accepted the urgency of the situation as Zuriko explained it. She said Darvin had asked her personally to choose someone, an expert, and who better than an old friend, the one everyone poured their heart out to. No, there was no time to lose, it had to be today. Yes, this afternoon. You must find out everything you can about what he did on the Outside. Yes, it's very important! Please, please Laia! Only you can do it! Don't worry, he's had a medical and a Watcher will be present. You'll be rendering a great service. Thank you so much, I'll never forget this, she had said overwhelmed with gratitude.

Laia did not have the heart to refuse. After all, they were both orphans and had once been like sisters despite... Her thoughts stopped there. She did not want to think about that. She had locked that memory away and had no wish to agonize over it again.

She was biting the inside of her lower lip as she glanced at the time. He'll be here any minute now, she groaned. Oh Codes! Why couldn't they have found a sex servicer to do this? Why in the name of Dovan had she agreed to it! Even if the clone hadn't caught anything, he was deconstructing. How could she have been so stupid! She gripped her head to stop from screaming out loud.

She got up to brush the mess she'd made of her hair. It may be important, she thought, but it has its down side. She put the brush down. Oh, she thought, the down side is so bad. She hoped it would not affect her reputation. Up to this point, she had risen through the ranks of the Aesthetics School from student to courtesan by dint of effort and talent. When she'd gained an A-class rank, she was independent of the School. The next step was to become the consort of a director or noble. Life then became so much easier. However, the request to become a consort could only come from a member of the Directorate. She knew Arron adored her and was not surprised when he asked her to become his consort. She happily accepted. He was a good man in every respect and she especially liked his gentleness. He had told her that the formal announcement would take time because he needed to follow the correct procedures. Arron was never one to rush, but she felt sure that he would soon be able to tell her the day of their civic declaration. But now? Here she was being thrown together with a clone! What in the name of Dovan would he think of this? How would he react? Would he know that the Chairman was behind the request? Oh, Codes, she whined. All I ever wanted was a place of peace and quiet since mama... She gulped.

Taking several deep breaths, she struggled to calm herself. She told herself to be positive and thought, if I succeed in getting the information they want, perhaps everything will be all right. But then, she shook her head. She had a bad feeling about this. Despite herself, she felt resentment swell up. Zuriko's a manipulator. How could you have forgotten? You're head in the clouds dreaming of a civic union with Arron! She doesn't have to give orders: she just ties you up in knots till you're so confused you don't know what you're doing.

A buzzer brought her crashing back to the present. She took a deep breath and went to the door. A screen above it showed a clone flanked by a Watcher. With a heavy heart, she opened the door.

'Good afternoon. As requested, here's the Packer,' Warton said, as he eyed Laia up and down. 'My orders are to wait outside,' he said, looking so frankly into her face that she felt offended. He then gave Ord a shove that sent him stumbling into the room. The Watcher gave Laia one last leer before closing the door.

Thinking of how crudely he'd stared, Laia was glad he'd not stayed. But when she turned and saw Ord standing with his arms hanging limply at his sides, she shuddered.

Ord gave a start. He recognised her. She was the beauty he had seen on that fateful day he had submitted the C80. Her long, shapely legs, well-proportioned figure, full-lipped, wide, sparkling blue eyes in a soft baby face were just as he remembered.

'Sit down,' Laia said with a faint smile, wondering if he would understand this simple request. Either way, she decided to get this over with as quickly as possible.

Ord stood motionless taking in his surroundings – the roundness of the room its saffron colours and subdued lighting.

How he wished his former self were here now. Today, and the day before, he had not eaten and his spirits were low, lower than he had ever known them to have been. Two Watchmen had come at the crack of dawn. They had pushed him round his room for breaking the order to remain in his clone district. The one who had brought him here had slapped him about the head. Unused to violence, Ord was terrified. But this? Why had they brought him to an A-class courtesan?

Laia was wondering why Ord had not moved. Looking at him, she thought he was neither good- nor bad-looking. He was in the middle, a sort of everyman. His hair was close-cropped and a sandy brown colour. His build was neither heavy nor light but in proportion to his height which was neither tall nor short. She could see from the hurt in his eyes that he had suffered. There was also a bewildered, hunted look about him that made her feel nervous. His sallow complexion and sunken cheeks bespoke a frail state of health. Poor clone, she thought, but quickly reminded herself that she had to get information, not sympathize. It was sympathy that got me into this mess in the first place, she reminded herself.

'Sit down,' she said, indicating a place on a sofa near the door on a lower level of the floor. 'Would you like something to drink?'

Ord moved to the spot she had gestured and sat, eyes cast downward.

'Would you like a drink?' she asked again, thinking he had not heard.

'Yes,' he replied, looking up momentarily.

After fixing him a healthy protein-rich drink and handing it to him, she stood in front of him, watching him take a few lacklustre sips. 'Cheer up,' she said sweetly. 'It's not the end of the world, you know. Look what a fine day it is,' she said, going to a window and pulling a curtain back.

'Do you watch the sun?' he asked.

'Watch it? Isn't that dangerous?' Laia said with a smile.

'It's life-light,' Ord answered.

'Do you watch it, then?' Laia asked, trying to coax him out of himself.

'Yes, mornings and evenings.'

'Did you watch it on the Outside, too?' she asked, sitting down on a chair opposite him. She knew she was broaching the subject far too quickly but didn't care. All she wanted was to get this over with.

Instead of answering, Ord said, 'I've seen you before.'

Surprised, Laia drew her head back a little and said, 'Oh, I don't think so...'

'Yes, it was almost a year ago. The day I submitted a C80. I was walking down the Hub stairway. I stopped. I decided to turn back. I was afraid. What I was doing was unclonelike, too individ.'

As Ord spoke, Laia noticed he was holding his glass with both hands so as not spill any. She wondered what his mental state was. She remembered there was something on the news about a clone going berserk. Was it him? She hoped not.

'I wish I'd turned back now,' he mumbled. 'If you hadn't come down the stairs I would've. It was your beauty that stopped me.'

Laia looked down. If it had not been for Ord's gentle tone, she would have called the Watcher. He did not speak in a threatening manner, but in the far away manner of the lost. She said nothing. She did not remember him, but she thought it might have been possible. She often used that staircase when she met Arron for lunch.

After a while, Ord continued: 'I didn't know what to do, so I filled in a C80. But what does it matter? Nobody cares. I carried on as best I could.' He stopped, put the glass down, held his head and began to sob.

Instinctively, Laia's hand reached out to him, but just as quickly she pulled it back. This is not going to be easy, she thought. He's in a bad way. She wondered if she ought to call the Watcher in.

After a few moments, she asked tenderly, 'Did we speak?'

'No,' choked Ord.

Laia got up and pushed some buttons. Some music began to play. 'This music may help you to relax,' she said.

Ord looked up at her. She was beautiful. But so was Eva and they had listened to music the last time they'd met. How he yearned for her.

Relieved at seeing him recover a little, Laia thought she would have one last try. 'Tell me about the Outside. You went out there, didn't you?'

Ord heard the lie behind the play-plea and realized in an instant why they had brought him here. He looked at Laia, now seated, fiddling with the folds of her dress as distress swept across her face. For a split second, he saw Eva's face appear between them. As it dissembled, his spirits sank with the realization that he would never see her again. He could hear Laia's sweet, coaxing voice. He shut his ears and eyes. He felt his head begin to spin – pictures, memories, faces, boxes, bits of this, fragments of that, until everything was spinning in the vortex of his mind's eye. Unable to bear it, he sank to his knees and clutched his head. Resembling a supplicant in a Renaissance painting, he looked up and howled from the pit of his being.

Laia had no need to call the Watchman. Warton was already signalling to her to open the door. He rushed in, grabbed Ord by the collar and dragged him out, pausing only, as he turned to close the door, to wink at Laia.

D AND Z

Darvin was in paroxysms of laughter.

'And to think, Q'zar didn't have an inkling of what we were up to! He, Director of Security!' It hurt so much he gripped his sides as he laughed.

Zuriko, glass in one hand and decanter in the other, was giggling so much she couldn't pour their drinks. 'Goes to show, he's no match for DeeDee,' she said to another roar of uncontrollable laughter. Then, trying to be a little more serious, she asked, 'But, D, tell me what news of Laia and that Ord.'

'What! You know the clone's name too! Have we no security here!' Darvin fell back, hooting at his joke.

'DeeDee,' she said again, not to be deflected from her purpose. 'Laia may not be one of my girls, but I did recommend her,' she pouted, offering Darvin his third strong drink.

'And so you did,' he replied, trying to sit up. 'I'm afraid it hasn't done her a lot of good. Arron was none too pleased to hear that she had been chosen for this special task. Did you know he was about to make a formal request to have her as his consort?'

'No,' Zuriko lied.

'Neither did I. Pity though. Don't know what he's going to do about it. By the way, I saw a film of the encounter. Attractive, very attractive. I'd not noticed her before. Never mind. But, you know, your idea...'

'Our idea,' corrected Zuriko.

'Our idea,' Darvin chimed back dutifully. 'It didn't work out as we'd hoped. The clone totally deconstructed. Q'zar didn't get much information, after all,' he gagged and once more roared with laughter.

'You mean the clone went gaga?' asked Zuriko, dabbing a handkerchief at her eyes that were wet with tears.

'Oh no, no, no,' said Darvin. 'But he did do something that was very different and we're still trying to figure it out. When he howled like an animal, what Valchek calls 'the primal scream', says it comes from the sub-cortical regions and is a cry for a god, he started to babble and, what's she called again?'

'Laia. A cry for a what?'

'Laia, right. A god, you know...'

'No, I don't. Here, let me top you up,' Zuriko said, taking his glass.

'Well, anyway, she was rather shaken as you can imagine by his grotesque performance. But he bawled out this word as he was dragged down the corridor. Q'zar noticed it when he watched the film. It's a word that's not been heard before. The superstition that people attach to signs! If you can't understand something, it's a sign! It never fails to surprise me. Anyway, Q'zar's looking into it – that should keep him busy!' Once more, they burst out laughing.

'That may explain why Laia seems so... unsettled recently,' said Zuriko, feigning concern. 'But how do they know it was a word and not just a...noise?'

'Oh, they know all right. They've got a voiceprint that proves he said it with intention. Oh, there's something else that Q'zar's busy with, which I think you should know about.'

'What's that?' said Zuriko, turning her back so that Darvin couldn't see how carefully she was listening.

'He wants to know which of his lieutenants leaked the information to one of your girls about the clone going to the Outside.' Darvin sat up, 'I'm afraid we'll have to tell him. Bad form not to.'

Zuriko had expected this question and had already formed a plan. Warton had taken Chu out that night and got him well tanked up and Zuriko had seen to it that one of her girls happened along as Chu wended an unsteady course homeward. The plan was to make out that Chu had divulged this information as a ploy to entice her home. 'Well,' she said, 'you know I don't like naming names.'

'I know,' replied Darvin sympathetically, 'but whoever it was, did divulge confidential information and was in breach of his duty, so I'm afraid...'

'Well, if I must.' Zuriko sighed. 'My girl tells me it was Chu. It was on his way home. She said he was all over her. He couldn't afford her so he offered information.'

'What is it about these girls of yours that makes every man tell them their secrets!' rued Darvin. 'I'll tell Q'zar. No need for you to get involved.' After a long pause, he added, 'It won't be long before he starts to try to get his own back,' and stared glumly into his empty glass.

Not wishing to remain in his cups, Darvin drew Zuriko so she sat astride his lap. 'What will you wear to the banquet? Oh, tell me ZeeZee, otherwise how shall I know you?'

'I shall not,' she answered, wagging a finger at him. 'You will have to search and find me,' she teased. Leaning forward, she sighed huskily, 'Oh, Dee, I'm so looking forward to it. Who will wear what? What performances we shall see! What dances we shall dance!' Looking up, she enthused, 'O Joypolis, jewelled city!'

As they talked on well into the night about the ball and banquet that would soon be upon them, they were aware that in every apartment both inside and outside of the Tower everyone was doing the same.

When Darvin slumped over and started snoring, Zuriko walked away from the sofa. She wanted to think how best she could set in motion the next part of her plan. She had to make sure that Laia was not on the guest list. But how? Rumour, she decided. Ugly rumours. Contact with a contaminated clone who had returned from the Outside with an evil sign upon his lips. She went into the other room, closed the door quietly and made one or two calls.

Valchek's Secret

Valchek leaned toward the mirror. How he had aged. He wished his skin was not so blotched and pockmarked. And his hair. How he wished it was thick and wavy. He took a comb and raked its wisps one way and then another until he found what he thought the best compromise. With a sigh, he got up and walked over to his wardrobe.

Sliding the door open, he thought everything's a compromise at my age. He ran his hand along an array of outfits. Thinking of the ball and banquet, he paused to pull those that took his fancy out. It was a tradition that nobles and directors had to conceal their identity. This was something he loved. Donning a mask always gave him the most delicious pleasure. He wondered why. He supposed it was the chance to be someone else. It freed him from the stuffy conventions he had to adhere to day in and day out. And he loved dressing up as a woman.

He took out last year's costume and pressed it against himself. He remembered how some citizens had mistaken him for Zuriko. But what he would never forget was how he had ordered a young clone to accompany him back to his apartment to help him alter his costume. He remembered the look of surprise on the clone's face when, taking off his headdress, he saw he was not a woman but a man. He could see he wanted to leave, but he ordered him to stay. Overawed by his status, the boy waited while he changed. Standing naked in front of him, he put the fear of the Codes into him by threatening to have him junked if he dared disobey. He smoothed the place on the bed where he had held him down and recalled the excitement of ravishing him.

Snapping out of his reverie, he told himself to tread carefully. The thought of the shame he would bring upon his family made him shudder. It was an offence for both citizens and nobles. But a noble cavorting with a clone! He knew he could get any number of handsome boys he liked at the *Adonis* or *The Bull's Milk*. But this was different. It was the power and domination that thrilled him. And, he added, affecting a regretful breath, the damnation he knew he had brought upon the clone.

Last year it all seemed so easy. Everything just fell into place. And no one, not even Q'zar, it seemed, suspected any wrong doing. That was the beauty of it, he thought. The clone began to deconstruct a month later, as he knew he would, because, like all the others, he had been coded for heterosexual behaviour. But what if the clone had uttered his name as he deconstructed? There had been nights when he had woken in a cold sweat at the thought. But as time passed and nothing happened, he believed he was in the clear.

This year he decided he would risk it again. Taking out another outfit, he held it against himself. He smiled. I shall win the gazes of all, he thought, and when the lights are dimmed, I shall seek out another sweet young thing to ravish upon the silk of my bed.

After he had chosen a costume, Valchek walked back to tidy up his study.

Recently, he had been researching the origin of several signs that could match the one that Ord had described in his C80. The most similar had been banned from use because it was the mark of the Andradist leader, Koron. Coincidence? Almost certainly. Even so, it was quite a discovery. He decided he would keep it to himself and only mention it if he needed to divert attention from himself. Yes, he thought, cocking his head to one side, I shall hold this information like a card in my hand and play it only if suspicion arises.

Remorse

It was early afternoon and Laia was walking slowly along the Midround corridor that marked the halfway point of the Tower. She had been shopping in the mall when a call came from Zuriko's secretary. It had been brief, but it had taken the spring out of her step. She moved to one side to get out of the way of people bustling past. Trying to untangle her thoughts, she gazed down at the streets. She then twisted her neck to look up at the Topround where a similar, though smaller ring circled the top of the Tower. It was where the Alzaris was. She wondered if Arron was there now. But no, it was too early for him, she thought as she turned away and continued to walk back to her apartment.

She had been informed that she had failed to make the clone reveal what he had seen and done on the Outside. The tone and brevity with which this was stated made it abundantly clear that certain individuals were not pleased. One was Zuriko. The other, though he was not mentioned by name, might be Darvin. She supposed she had failed. Unused to criticism, especially harshness, she felt hurt.

The secretary even had the audacity to suggest she should have appealed to his sexual instincts. They shouldn't have asked me in the first place, she thought recalling her fear of being so close to a clone who had crossed to the Outside. They should have got a sex servicer. She might have coaxed it out of him. Though, I doubt it. He was too far gone. Recalling how he had howled, she shook her head and quickened her step.

As she turned off the main thoroughfare into the quieter corridor that led to her apartment, she knew her reputation was in jeopardy. Not only had she failed to get the information they wanted, but a rumour was going around. People were saying the clone hadn't had a medical and that he'd must have met barbarians because he'd howled a name. If this were true... Had Zuriko lied to her? She shuddered to think what Arron was thinking. Tears welled up. She had not heard from him since meeting the clone. He had not answered her calls. There was even talk she might not be on the guest list for the banquet.

Once the door to her apartment came into view, she broke into a half run. Reaching it, she slammed her hand against the ID pad and, as soon as the door unlocked, rushed in and burst into a flood of tears.

She hated Zuriko for this. She couldn't rationalise it, but she felt she had been used. Fool, she thought, pushing her hands into her thick blonde hair to clutch her head. Truth is you have always been used. Only this time, you have been used against yourself. She took several deep breaths to try to calm down. Yes, she was pretty. Some said beautiful. And no, she was neither clever nor cunning, nor spiteful – none of those things you had to be to climb the ladder of success. She hoped Arron understood this. But, oh what a fool she'd been to believe Zuriko. But what else could she have done? She trusted people and did not want to believe they were wicked and conniving. But why, why did she do this?

This question made her stare hard, first one way then another. Why me? She's not interested in Arron. She has Darvin. Was it just chance? Or the past? Her mother was more to blame than my father, she thought. She did not want to go over all that again. It was too painful. Her mother's brutal, senseless murder had left her with a profound sense of loss. She knew she could never overcome that loss. She would live forever as a child cocooned within the love that her mother surrounded her in. This, she decided, was how she would keep her mother alive. Could Zuriko be seeking revenge, she wondered, wringing her hands and catching sight of her tortured expression in a mirror as she stood up.

Going into an adjoining room she filled a glass with water. As she drank, she felt calmer, though her face was still puffed from crying. As usual, she thought, I don't know what to do. I'm just a pawn in what may be a game. But I don't even know if it is a game or who the players may be or even if they exist. If only I were clever like Arron!

She put down the glass and decided the best thing she could do was take a walk in Happiland Park. She always found it cheered her up. It was a place that conjured up many happy childhood memories.

***

By the time Laia reached the big, bright, gaudy gates of Happiland, Joypolis' largest park, it was mid-afternoon. Despite the sunshine, there were very few people about.

As she walked a spotless pink path, she was thinking how Happiland used to be so popular. Most people did not think there was any point in going there once they had been a few times. They preferred donning a cyber-helmet at the game centres. In recent years, it had become a talking point: should it be replaced? If so, with what?

Not a week went by without some new idea for its space. Laia hoped it would remain forever. She remembered how her mother used to bring her here often.

Yes, she recalled, that's where we used to play peek-a-boo and hide-and-seek. What wonderfully simple games. Not power games. Her mind shot to Arron. Why hadn't he rung her? She'd rung several times. Each time his secretary took the call and said she'd pass on her message as soon as he got back.

Looking around, she could see row upon row of plastic trees, bushes and flowers. Their leaves and flowers vibrated with laser. The bark of the trees was an earthy brown, more real than the real it was said. The flowers would open as you approached, triggering hidden sensors to release fragrances and laser images of butterflies and humming birds.

Over to her right she saw several paddle boats on an artificial lake. They bobbed up and down, jostling one another as if to say use me. She smiled and headed toward them. As she did so, a deer appeared at the edge of a nearby copse. It gazed at her with great soft eyes and then shyly ran back into the shade. She knew it, as well as everything else here, was only an image. That's why it was all so beautiful. The real thing would have been horrible. Here, everything is beautifully clean, she thought.

Reaching the jetty, she marvelled at the play of laser light upon the lake. Sometimes green, sometimes blue, with crocodile and hippopotami shapes erupting from the water's surface at a distance where they could be properly viewed. She stepped into a small yellow paddle boat with the curious name 'Liberty'. Instead of choosing automatic, she pushed manual.

As she pedalled, the image of pink flamingo taking flight made the day's events seem less important. Happiland, she thought, you're doing it again. It had never failed to send her into raptures of delight. She decided she would abandon herself to fate. After all, what was the worst that could happen? Time would pass and all would be forgotten. Fortune would favour her again. She braved a smile. And if the unthinkable happened and she was not on the list for the banquet, she would come here. Happiland would always be here, she mused, trying to hide her disappointment.

Still hurting at Arron's silence, she paddled toward some reeds. She remembered how her mother would always whisper on passing the reeds, 'Tell me if you see any crocodiles, won't you?' as if they were real and dangerous! What a laugh, she thought.

Passing the reeds, she saw a crocodile slip off a bank and sink into the lilac-tinted water. As she paddled on, an odd shape caught her eye. She pedalled toward it. As she drew closer, she began to doubt her eyes. Surely it couldn't be real? She paddled slowly closer, hoping it would disappear. But it didn't. She stopped pedalling and stared at it. It looked like an arm. How ugly, she thought. So white and sticking up like that. How in the Codes could it have got there?

Paddling back to the jetty, she decided she would report it. Before doing so, she took a last long look back to make doubly sure it was not an illusion. She still did not know whether it was real or not but, either way, it should be reported. It looked like an arm. It was horrible. She flipped her telecom open and, even before she pushed the single key to contact Security, she knew if that was an arm, it would be big news.

An Arm

Four Watchers stood around a coroner's slab upon which lay a severed arm. It was crinkled and the colour of pig's tripe, bar the inky blue bruises on the bicep and forearm. The hand was crumpled and the fingers stuck up stiffly.

'Whose arm is it?' asked Q'zar, transfixed by the grisly sight and addressing no one in particular.

'At the moment, we have no idea,' Warton replied, taking the lead in answering since Chu had been arrested for leaking the information about Ord's visits to the Outside. Inwardly, he smirked at his success. Not only had he escaped detection, but he had got Zuriko to agree to his demand for an A-class courtesan as his reward. He had named the woman who found this arm.

'It's imperative we find out,' said Q'zar, 'And quickly. All clones are accounted for, correct?' he snapped, his eyes still glued to the arm.

'Yes, Domo,' replied Warton, beginning to relish his new role. 'All clones are accounted for and no citizen has been any reported as missing.'

'How quickly can we get a forensic analysis?' Q'zar asked, this time directing his question at Braun, Chu's replacement.

'By tomorrow afternoon we shall know exactly whose arm it is, Domo,' came Braun's response. He was on the point of adding that the Watchers would have the murderer behind bars before you could say Dovan the Great but checked himself, remembering he had only just been promoted.

'The arm is badly bruised here. And look,' Q'zar pointed, 'see how bloated and puckered it is. How long was it in the lake? Make sure they give a time. These three fingers look broken. We need to know when this happened. It may not be as recent as we suspect. Although chemicals in the lake may have...' Q'zar's voice petered out as he realized the futility of conjecture. 'You say the lake is being dredged?'

'Yes, Domo,' Warton replied. 'If anything is found, you shall be informed at once.'

'If they find nothing, have them search the entire park.'

'Yes, Domo.'

'What I can't understand is how this arm was dislocated. It has not been cut off. Could it have been torn off? Get forensics to answer that, too. It's not humanly possible to tear an arm off. Animals? Could an animal have roamed into the city? Highly unlikely. Can't rule it out, though.' No one answered. 'We need a detailed analysis of this and quickly too. Get it to the laboratory at once.'

'Yes, Domo,' Hersh replied, drawing a black plastic bag from beneath the slab and placing it beside the arm. He drew on a pair of surgical gloves before placing the arm into the bag. Sealing the bag with a tape, he bowed and headed for the door. Just as he reached it, Q'zar barked another order.

'Tell forensics this is a priority and not a word is to get out. Is that understood?' He glared at each lieutenant in turn. 'If I so much as hear a whisper of this, the person responsible will be behind bars a lot longer than Chu. Is that clear!'

'Yes, Domo,' all three shouted in unison.

When Hersh left the room, Warton and Braun went back to their desks and busied themselves, pretending not to notice Q'zar pacing up and down. Behind his back they exchanged furtive glances. They had never seen him as rattled as this.

Q'zar suddenly felt the need for space to think. The only place for him at times like this was either the Watchtower or the Practice Hall. He was about to leave the room when he stopped and said, 'I want all Watchers placed on full alert. Anything new...anything,' he repeated, 'contact me immediately.'

'Yes, Domo.' Both Watchers jumped to their feet and clicked their heels.

'While we're waiting for forensics, I want that deconstructed clone taken to the Encrypt. He's a suspect. Only a madman could tear an arm off. It's highly unlikely that a deranged clone could do this, but it's the only lead we have at the moment.' Scowling, he added, 'He won't be going to the Outside anymore.'

As he turned to go, Warton indicated that he wished to speak.

'What is it?' Q'zar snapped.

'Respectively, Domo, I suggest that the citizen who made this discovery be placed under immediate house arrest. She may talk to Media.'

Q'zar considered this for a moment.

'It's an odd way to reward a citizen's diligence, but I see your point. If Media got whiff of this, we'd risk having a panic on our hands. Permission granted. Explain the reasons to her and, remember Warton, she's a high-ranking courtesan. Make sure she has every comfort she requires and understands that this is only a temporary measure.'

'Yes, Domo.'

When the door slammed shut behind Q'zar, Warton turned to face the mirror on the wall. He combed his oiled black hair back, first on the left then on the right side. As he did so, he told himself, no woman can resist those blue eyes.

***

Q'zar stepped into the stillness of the Practice Hall. At the far end, a pale milky glow shone down upon the bust of the founder. He slipped his sandals off before crossing the white tatami mats to bow before the bust. He then sat as still as a stone with the soles of his feet tucked beneath him. 'Murder,' he said to himself. His hands, which lay palms up resting upon his knees, twitched involuntarily. He focussed upon a spot forward of his knees and put his mind on the movement of his breath to calm himself.

As the turmoil inside began to abate, he began to think: the report should be ready tomorrow. Forensics may say it was an accident. Fine. But if they have no explanation, it'll have to be treated as a crime. In which case, I'll have to call an emergency meeting. But the day before the banquet? Damn, he swore, knowing Darvin would never agree to that.

Though it galled him, he realized he could not risk any further loss of political influence. If he demanded a meeting, it would create a storm of protest and play directly into the hands of his opponents. He resigned himself to having to sit on the results till the day after the banquet. But he would send a report to all the directors straightaway. He would outline how the matter stood at the moment and add that, pending forensics' findings, everyone should be prepared to attend an emergency meeting the morning after the banquet. He would also demand that Media remain silent until the matter had been fully discussed.

As he tried to calm his mind, he wondered what Arron would think of Laia's house arrest. The last thing I need is Arron joining the rest against me. Surely he can understand that security must come first. I'll explain it to him personally. Who knows, maybe he's changed his mind about her. Agreeing to meet a clone in her apartment! How could she have been so stupid.

Unable to focus his thoughts, he got up and walked across to a rack of swords. Taking one, he lifted it and looked along the timeless curve of its blade. Then, making a few cuts and thrusts, he stopped and felt the weight and balance of the sword appreciatively. Holding it, he thought of Chu. He missed him. He was his right-hand man. He intended to hand the department over to him when he retired. How could he do such a thing? He let the end of the sword fall. He felt uneasy about his verdict on Chu. There was no hard evidence, only the word of one of Zuriko's girls. But all fingers pointed to Chu and even Chu could not swear that he had not blurted out something. And yet, even in saying that, Chu had shown his honest nature. I trusted him, he thought. I know how he holds his sword. I have seen him on this mat a thousand times. It doesn't ring true.

After making a few cuts, he paused and thought of Warton. He's come out of this rather well. A gunman. Nothing wrong with that but, it's different. You're removed, can't see the enemy. And there are rumours about him. Seems he enjoys beating girls. Hardly fitting behaviour for a Watchman. Have to talk to him about it. Lifting the sword, turning it and seeing it glint, Q'zar wondered if he had detected a note of pleasure in Warton's voice when he'd agreed to place Laia under house arrest. Slowly, he turned and moved to the centre of the mat where he began to execute a series of lightning cuts. Soon, all that could be seen in the dim light were flashes of tempered steel above a shadowy figure.

Junked

Ord was waiting for the first hint of dawn to appear when a tap at the door made him turn. He wondered who it could be at such an early hour. Opening the door, he saw two Watchmen. As they stepped in, he stepped back.

One of them produced some papers and formally requested him to accompany them, muttering something about compliance with applicable conditions. Ord knew it would be futile to resist. As he looked around his room, it struck him it might be the last time he would ever see it. A sense of loss filled him. It wasn't much, but it was home and felt like a part of him. He gulped, took his jerkin, picked up his rucksack and followed one Watcher out as the other locked the door behind them. Seeing him check if the door had locked, Ord knew he would not be coming back.

The Watcher said, 'This way.' Ord followed. The only sound that could be heard were their footsteps squeaking on the recently polished corridor floor. For Ord, everything, even the scuffs and scratches on the wall, seemed to take on a new aura of importance. It grieved him as each familiar sight passed before his eyes so quickly.

Outside, nothing looked different. But spaces that he had known for years looked as if they were about to dissemble before his eyes. After he'd been dragged out of Laia's room, he knew this day was not far off. He had imagined what it would be like many times. Yet now he was living it, it felt different.

The Watchmen motioned him to board a grey bus that was parked outside. As he climbed in, another pointed to where he was to sit. He sat down and looked out the window that was protected on the outside by wire mesh. After a few seconds, the bus began to purr and glide silently through the brightening darkness. It took a circuitous route past the Stadium, Game City, Happiland Park, Dovan Square until it reached the district in which the Encrypt stood.

When it came to a stop in front of the main gates, the Watchers got up. One told Ord to stand and follow him, the other followed as he was led off.

As Ord stumbled out, a guard was opening a door in the gate of the Encrypt. Ord looked at the trees in the distance. He could see the sun had not risen above them yet but that its rays were splayed out behind them. A guard nudged him forward, rolling his eyes at what he imagined to be Ord's deranged state of mind. The guard who held the door open, screwed a finger at his temple as Ord stepped through.

Once inside, Ord was led toward a rectangular building. It was identical in shape, but not height, to other buildings that were ranged alongside it. Looking from side to side, Ord was surprised he could not see any clones. Perhaps, it was too early he thought. Maybe they're all having breakfast. Seeing the tip of the sun appear above the trees, he stopped. The Watcher behind shoved him forward.

Once through the double doors, Ord was led to a counter behind which a clerk sat. The clerk placed some forms in front of him and pointed to a pen. Ord took the pen from its stand and began to fill them in. After filling in his name and some other details, his mind went blank. What was his telecom number, the address of the Carer Clone Station he'd been trained at years ago and his locator number? Surely they know all this, he thought. Not a word was spoken as he filled in as many sections as he could. When he looked up, he noticed the Watchmen had gone and two guards had taken their place. One of them smirked when he said he couldn't answer half of the questions.

Hearing this, the clerk said, 'That'll do,' and took the form. The guard then said, 'This way,' and led him along a bare corridor to a grey door numbered 103. Unlocking it, he gestured Ord to enter. Ord went in. As he did so, the door was closed behind him. He stood for a few seconds, looking at the door, imagining he could hear its echo. When he could no longer hear it, the silence that followed was so profound it unnerved him. He looked around the room. There was no window. He walked toward the single bed and sat on it. It was hard. He looked at the white walls and the hole in the corner that was, he supposed, a toilet. The only furniture was the bed and the small table beside it. What is this, he wondered.

As time began to hang ever more heavily, he began to grow more anxious. He had not imagined this. He'd thought there would be other clones. Perhaps, they'll come later and take me to another building where there are clones, he thought. It'd be wonderful to see Krm again. It has been so long since we've seen each other. He strained his ears but could hear nothing outside. He wondered how long he would have to wait before they explained what was going on.

In the prolonged and unchanging silence, he closed his eyes. He saw trees. Sunlight was filtering through them. He was walking beneath them. He wished he had never returned. He should have stayed out, he thought. He got up and began to pace up and down as he grew ever more restless waiting for someone to come. He was on the point of beating against the door and calling for someone to bring water when he heard the tip-tap of metal-capped shoes. The door opened and the guard stepped in bearing a tray. He placed it upon the table. Ord was on the point of asking when he would be taken to join other clones when, distracted by the smell of the food, he sat down. They had taken him before he'd eaten breakfast. When he looked up, the guard had gone. Shaking his head, he tucked into the food wondering if this was lunch.

After thirty minutes, the guard returned and took the tray away. Feeling better after having eaten, Ord decided to say nothing. He had not forgotten the beating he had got from the Watcher who had taken him to be questioned. He decided to wait till they took him to join the others.

For the rest of the day, he alternated between sitting, lying, standing and pacing up and down. How he wished there was a window. It seemed to him that the morning had passed more quickly than the afternoon, but now time weighed so heavily it was driving him insane.

After what seemed an eternity, once more he heard the tip-tapping of an approaching guard. The door opened and the guard entered with what he imagined must be his dinner. Ord was on the point of demanding to know what was going on, when the guard, not the same person who had brought his lunch, gave him such a mean look that he fell silent. Eyeing him, he placed the tray, stared at him for a full minute, before walking away and slamming the door as he left.

After eating, the silence returned. Ord felt desperate. The air was dry and he felt thirsty. He lay back and fell into an uneasy sleep.

He dreamt he was lying in a small boat drifting on a glassy sea. It wasn't a real sea. It was the sea that the Desert Island Game began with. He did not know how long he had been in the boat, only that he was dying of thirst and that his eyes stung and his head hurt. The water in the boat sploshed from side to side, the coolness of its sound taunting rather than comforting. The relentless heat of the sun bore down on his back and made him wonder if the game player had forgotten him. Slowly, he became aware that the sounds beneath the boat had changed. The boat was no longer bobbing and he could hear waves breaking up ahead. Pulling himself up, he peered over the prow and saw a tropical reef. Water, he begged the game player, water. Though his eyes stung from salt, he could just make out a yellow sandbar. He sank back and waited for the boat to reach it.

Feeling it bump and jostle up against the shore, he heaved himself up, half fell out and staggered across the sand to the welcoming shade of palm trees. As he stepped into their coolness, he stopped dead. He could see a face staring out of the dark green foliage. He blinked. It was still there. It was his own face and, yet, the face of a savage. It stared at him without recognition. Wild without reason, reason without cause...

Ord awoke and sat bolt upright as if the words were a clarion call from a distant land. He looked daggers at the door. I'm thirsty, I must drink. Controlling his instinct to rush at the door and hammer upon it, he got up and moved cat-like toward it. He placed his ear against it. He could hear the muffled voices of the guards down the corridor. Slowly, he turned the handle and pulled on it lightly. To his surprise, it was not locked. As it opened inwardly, he doubted they would notice. Holding it ajar, he could hear what they were saying.

'Anyone know when he's going to be junked?'

'Nope. All we've been told is to hold him. Day after the big party's my bet.'

'Yeah,' replied a third. 'Would've been today hadn't it been for all the la-di-dahs dressing up. If it had been today, we could've gone, right?'

'Get on! Who'd invite you, eh?' They laughed.

'I've heard something's up. That's why they want to hold him. Make the sub talk before we put him out of his misery. It's something to do with what's going on in Happiland. Don't ask me what, but it's got Q'zar rattled.'

'Well, if they want us to beat the shit out of him, I don't mind. Make up for missing all the celebrations. They don't feel anything anyway. Brainless babblers, that's what they are. Did you see him staring at the sky when we brought him in? I ask you, what an airhead. Didn't even know his own ID, I ask you!'

'Yeah, it's sad, but it can't be helped. We can't have head cases wandering around, can we? A mercy killing is the best thing.'

Hearing this, Ord let go of the door. If he was pale before, now he had turned a deathly shade. *They're going to kill me.* He pressed both hands hard together and took several deep breaths to stop himself from going to pieces. After some false starts, he started to get a hold of himself. *That's why the door isn't locked,* he thought. *They think I'm a head case. They want me to walk out so they can beat the shit out of me!*

Ord was unaware that up to now all the clones who had been brought to the Encrypt had suffered severe mental breakdowns. His deconstruction had been different. Instead of becoming dysfunctional, his visits to the Outside as well as Eva's friendship had been therapeutic. When he finally broke down, his primal scream had completely erased his conditioning. On waking the following morning, he felt different but at peace. He was reborn. The Watchers could not detect this change because it was new and, therefore, unsought. Other events had also distracted them, not least the discovery of a severed arm.

Ord carefully closed the door. He sat down and began to think hard. He must escape. Escape could mean only one place: the forest. How would he survive? He remembered the stream. Water, I will have. Shelter, I will make. It will do. Food? I shall scavenge the tips, and, if they see me, who would dare take chase, who would dare follow me to the Outside? None. He gave a snort of contempt, a gesture that was entirely new to his repertoire of body language. He would become the Man in his dream. 'Yes,' he cried, feeling his blood rise as a scowl twisted his face. 'And I will kill, as they would kill me.' He stared coldly at the door. There was only one question left: When?

The Banquet

There were only two ways to enter the banquet hall. Directors had to descend one of three stairways from an upper floor, citizens by one of five entrances on the Midround.

The first to appear were a group of clones who had been selected from a total of six hundred thousand. They had been told to arrive first. They wore a smarter version of their usual uniformed attire – navy blue, high-necked tunics of a light cotton material with the insignia of Joypolis emblazoned on a breast pocket. It was never made clear to them whether they had been invited as helpers or guests. Most of them did not mind the ambiguity. They deemed it a privilege to be there in whatever capacity. Media did little to clarify the situation by only hinting at recognition of hard work.

Soon, groups of citizens began to arrive. Most were childless couples, but there were also some family groups. On entering, the youngest would rush off to join friends of a similar age. But the liveliest arrivals were single men and women who looked as if they had come from another party. They were dressed in the latest fashions and gazed with rapturous delight at the sumptuous décor.

Row upon row of scintillating chandeliers hung from an ornate ceiling upon which were embossed the heroes and heroines of Joypolis. Paintings that were considered masterpieces of the various schools of art that had flourished in the city decorated the walls of the rotunda. In the alcoves between the paintings, there stood statues of former chairmen, scientists, artists, engineers, and inventors. At the centre of the rotunda stood the buffet stands – a pagoda for Chinese cuisine, a chateau above the offerings of French cuisine and an elephant housing Indian food.

As guests began to pour into the ballroom, soft music accompanied the familiar voices of the Founders making famous speeches. Soon the rotunda was packed and, as guests began to circulate, lively conversation bubbled up interspersed with bursts of laughter. When the Master of Ceremonies began to call upon well-known figures to make speeches, attention shifted to the stage upon which they stood. Just as the younger guests were beginning to tire of their speeches, the lights of the buffet stands lit up to show they were ready to begin serving.

Against this backdrop, nobles and directors began to descend the staircases as if from Olympus. They all wore the most extravagant costumes and it was impossible to tell from a distance who they were. As the citizens stood about nibbling hors d'oeuvres, a great gasp went up from one quarter. Everyone turned. There, descending the east stairway, was an extraordinary figure. Though no one could be sure, they imagined it was Sovran or even Lara.

Valchek was delighted to have won the first accolade. Wearing a burgundy red quilted garment held together by silver clasps that ran diagonally from his right shoulder down, he tiptoed down the stairway. Dark lace covered his arms and hands and silver bracelets adorned his wrists. A short pleated black cape covered his shoulders and a light helmet with a hologram pattern moving across it concealed his identity.

There were several more gasps of admiration for the daring fashion of nobles and directors, but none eclipsed Valchek's. He had timed his entrance perfectly: it was neither too early nor too late.

Soon, the floor was cleared of buffet stands and as strains of music were heard and multi-coloured lights swirled across the floor, a great cheer went up. Everyone rushed onto the dance floor. The party had begun.

Through this kaleidoscope of colour, music and wild abandon, Valchek walked seeking an attractive young clone. As he did so, the edge of his helmet began to rub against his neck. He tried to push the top of his cape under it. But it continued to tear at his skin. He decided he would have to go back to his apartment to fix it.

He decided to leave by the Midround rather than be seen climbing the stairs. His ears were still booming from the music as he stepped into an elevator. Reaching the Topround, he lifted the helmet up to stop it rasping against his neck as he walked toward his apartment.

When he closed the door to his apartment, he unclipped the helmet and took hold of it ready to lift it off quickly. He winced when the tender skin beneath stretched and snapped as he pulled it off. He put the helmet down and went to fix a drink. Slopping vermouth into the first glass that came to hand, he gulped it down. As he banged the glass down with a long exhalation, the doorbell chimed. Startled, he went back into the adjoining room to view who it could be. The screen showed the capped and uniformed shoulders of a clone.

Valchek was dumbfounded: what in the Name of the Codes was a clone doing unaccompanied on the Topround! It was expressly forbidden. Only nobles and directors occupied the Topround. Furious, he opened the door and shouted at the clone to explain himself. On seeing his face, he froze. This was no clone. This was a...

Before he was able to finish his thought, a metal hand clamped his throat, lifted him, entered and shook him like a doll. One of his high-heeled shoes flew off and clunked in the corner as his neck snapped.

Now or Never

Ord realized that this night would provide him with his best and only chance of escape. It was the night of the banquet. He knew from previous years that the streets would be deserted because everyone would be at home glued to their screens. Watchers would also be assigned to duties at the Tower. If he could only get past the guards, he felt sure he could reach the perimeter. He had seen how close the trees were to the far wall when they brought him into the compound. But how could he slip past the guards? He decided to wait until the laser show that marked the beginning of the end of the celebrations began.

He felt certain that when it started to depict the history of Joypolis by projecting images into the night sky, the guards would go out to watch. As each picture faded, it would be punctuated by a great fanfare that would drown out every other sound. Ord knew the whole show would last twenty-four minutes. The twelfth picture marked the climax and, when it faded, guests would begin to leave the Tower. He closed his eyes and tried to picture the surrounding wall, its height and where he should try to scale it.

If a guard came, he decided it would best to play dumb. If he spoke, he might rouse suspicion and they might lock the door. The thought of that door being locked made him gaze upward and plead for luck. Better, he thought, to lull them into a sense of false security. Let them think I am some kind of vegetable.

When the guard came with his supper, Ord sat staring into the empty space in front of him. He felt his stomach sink when he became aware of another guard outside. The guard banged the tray down on the bedside table. Ord did not flinch. When the guard shouted, 'Eat up, head case! It may be your last,' Ord made no reply. The guard left the room, shaking his head, 'Nuts,' he said to the other before slamming the door shut.

Ord's nerves were stretched to breaking point when, hearing them walking away, he crept to the door. Looking down the narrow gap between the door and its frame, he could see no bolt. He gave a great sigh of relief before turning back to eat. As he ate, he figured from the time he'd seen on the guard's wrist watch he'd have to wait another hour before the laser show began.

An hour later, Ord began to wonder if he had made a mistake. Maybe he couldn't hear the laser show. He began to pace up and down. He was beginning to sweat and wonder whether he should try to get out now or stick to his plan when he heard an explosion followed by a fanfare. His shoulders sank with relief. He knew that same sound would be deafening outside.

He took a deep breath, wiped the sweat from his brow and moved to the door. Putting his ear to it, he listened carefully. He could hear nothing. With bated breath, he turned the handle and opened the door a fraction. He knew it could not be seen from the outside as it opened inward. As the fanfare faded, voices from the end of the corridor became audible. At first, he could not make out what they were saying but, gradually, he caught snatches.

'Hey guys, take a look at this!'

Ord reckoned there must be three guards on duty. Whether they were the same he had seen earlier he was not sure, though he reckoned they might be because the guard who had brought his supper was the same who had brought his dinner. He hoped they were, because they would have been on duty for double their normal shift.

'D'you reckon one of us ought to keep an eye on airhead?'

Ord could not hear the reply. It was drowned in a fanfare of trumpets, followed by an enormous boom. He strained his ears. Hearing nothing, he took several deep breaths to control the tension that was pouring sweat out of every pore. He knelt down at the edge of the door and peeped down the corridor. He couldn't see anyone. It looked deserted. He could see his rucksack still hanging on the chair where he'd signed the forms. He got up and with his heart beating crazily, stepped into the corridor. Looking up and down, he walked quickly toward the entrance, keeping close to the wall. If someone suddenly appeared, he knew there was nowhere he could hide.

As he drew close to the reception area, he crouched down and crept past in case someone was in the office. As he passed the chair in front of the desk, he lifted his rucksack off and noticed there was no one in the office. He stood up as he stepped behind the doors to the entrance.

The right door was open, the left, behind which he stood, closed. He pulled his rucksack on as he crouched down. He could hear the guards talking outside. He pressed himself hard against the edge of the door before leaning out to get a look. Seeing three of them standing beside a ventilator shaft off to his right, he pulled his head back. They were about five metres away gazing at the Tower with their backs to him. One was pointing at a huge mosaic of Dovan the Great, holding the Book of the Illustrious Codes. Ord waited for the next one to appear with its accompanying fanfare.

When it did, he decided it was now or never. Seeing them pointing up at it, his heart was hammering against his ribs as he stood up, slunk out and slid behind the left wall of the portico. He knew he could not be seen there. He flattened himself against the wall ready for the next move – to reach and turn the corner of the building. He waited until he heard a guard holler, 'Whoa! Look at that!' In the next instant, music began to blare as the picture revolved. His heart in his mouth, Ord tiptoed toward the corner of the building. Turning it, he stopped. At first, he could hear nothing but music. But as it faded, he could hear the guards. His heart was pounding. He wondered if they would go back inside. He didn't wait to find out. He loped toward the far end of the building, ducking beneath each window he passed.

On reaching the end of the building, the light cast by the previous picture had vanished and Ord could only just make out the dark shape of the compound wall. He knew he was out of sight of the guards and that in a second or two, the fanfare that marked the beginning of the next picture would deafen any sound his attempt to scale it might make. When the fanfare burst forth, he ran full pelt toward the wall. Reaching it, he hunched down before leaping up high enough to grip the top and clamber over. He let himself hang till he could see if the ground beneath was clear. Letting go, he landed softly on artificial grass. Looking from side to side, he could see no one. He turned and began to run as close to the wall as possible. When he reached the intersection, he crouched in the shadows and scanned the three streets opposite. Seeing no one, he turned right and raced toward the perimeter.

As he ran, he could hardly believe his luck. Had he really done it? Had he really escaped? He felt as high as a kite. He reached the perimeter just as the next picture was unfolding. This time it was the twelve members of the Great Council. Their faces formed a ring that symbolized unity of purpose and afforded just enough light for Ord to see the ground at his feet. He ran stumbling across the rough no man's land between the perimeter and the trees. His chest was heaving as he reached the cover of trees. He knew there were eight more pictures to go. Looking into the deep shadows between the trees, he smiled as he began to search for a place to rest before the last light faded.

Emergency

There are moments in every life that are critical. They can feel like crossroads in the way they compel a decision as to which direction to take. As Q'zar stood upon the Watchtower in the pale primrose light of early morning, he felt the weight of such a decision. Seeing the sun shoot its first bright lances, his hawk-like features drew tighter as he wracked his brains for an explanation of the events of the previous forty-eight hours.

He felt stunned. A clonicide. The first ever. Then this... He shook his head in disbelief as he eyed the report he had placed on the bench behind him. Forensics had confirmed that the arm belonged to a clone called Url. Of that, there could be no doubt. DNA had proven it. It was the same clone who had suggested changes to the way goods should be stacked at the Hub. Coincidence? Q'zar shook his head. He had no idea.

The prompt completion of the report had given him time to contact Darvin and get his begrudging permission to call an emergency meeting on the morning after the banquet. He knew no one would thank him for this. Darvin had gone on endlessly about how everyone would be tired and in no mood for a meeting. After all, it was only a clone. Surely it could wait, he had pleaded. He had made every conceivable objection until Q'zar lost his temper and yelled that it was just not that simple. Only then did he dither and mutter that a brief meeting might be possible.

Q'zar knew his political career was at stake. If Url's murder turned out to be inexplicable and there were no further incidents, then he would have to step down. Even the few allies he could muster would not forgive him this. He sucked the cold air between his teeth as he weighed the implications. But no, all his training told him that to delay would be a grave error.

How, in the Name of the Codes, he swore, could Darvin cite tiredness as a reason not to call a meeting? Slapping his hands down onto the rail, he blamed it on so many years of peace. It had lulled everyone into a false sense of security. How, he wondered, can I make them see the seriousness of the situation? The thought that those who would resent this meeting most were members of his own class made Q'zar survey the streets below with a sense of foreboding.

Now, as if murder were not enough, the main suspect had escaped. Q'zar had hoped to inform the meeting that a suspect had been arrested. The clone had a motive: he was deconstructing because of Url's new rules and had taken revenge. He did not believe Ord was the murderer, but intended to use him as a decoy. The stupidity of the guards! He clenched his teeth in an effort to control his rage. While they pledged allegiance drinking toast after toast outside, the clone had walked free!

Ord's untimely escape had placed Q'zar in an awkward position. To convince the committee that the draconian measures he wished to introduce were needed, he had to be seen as above reproach. Any admittance of negligence would give them just the excuse they needed to undermine his authority. He decided he would say nothing about Ord. In any case, he would soon be caught. Unless he's gone to the Outside, he thought, tilting his head at this possibility.

But then, recalling the main issue, he told himself he had to get everyone on the committee behind him. Feeling the burden of responsibility weigh even heavier, he turned, picked up the forensics report and left the Watchtower thinking, if I fail, I fear for this city.

***

Q'zar was the first to reach the committee room. The door was open so he entered and stood at the far end of the room. As he waited, all the instincts of his training as a security expert told him something was threatening Joypolis. He did not believe a clone could be the perpetrator. He had ordered his arrest to distract Media. He sensed the truth was something far, far worse. Forensics stated that the arm had been torn off with a force that was not human. The report was unable to specify what could have torn it off, but noted that teeth and claw marks were absent. Traces of a metallic substance suggested a machine. What, in the name of Dovan the Great, could it be?

After he had calmed himself, Q'zar returned to pick up the thread of his thought. Whatever it is, it's roaming the streets, he said to himself. NewsTalk can't have this. They'd blow it out of all proportion. Could cause a panic and that's the last thing we need. How much of the report should be divulged, he wondered.

Before he could answer that question, someone entered the room. Turning, Q'zar saw it was Gorvik. They nodded to one another and were about to exchange a few words when the others came shuffling in led by Darvin. They were laughing about the previous night's revelry. If only they knew, thought Q'zar, noticing one or two yawning between laughs. As they went to their seats, it became clear that everyone was present except Valchek and O. It was unusual for Valchek to be late, thought Q'zar. And how could O not bother to attend an emergency meeting!

Once seated, Q'zar looked at each person around the table. Darvin's face was puffed from drink and lack of sleep. Even Arron, usually a paragon of moderation, looked off colour. Probably worried about that Drovny woman, he thought. Not a lot I can do about that right now. He looked over at Sovran. She sat sphinx-like, her intelligent brow raised, waiting for an explanation. Like a vulture, he thought. Beside her sat the only other woman on the committee – Lara. She was trying to stifle a yawn. What a contrast to Sovran, he thought. Only Gorvik and Sovran looked their usual alert selves. But where was Valchek?

After everybody had settled down, Darvin cleared his throat. He looked at his watch. He, too, was puzzled at Valchek's absence. Must have drunk too much, he thought. Shrugging his shoulders, he began to speak.

'Ahem, I think we had better begin without the Head of Personnel. Doubtless, he'll be along shortly. Probably having some difficulty deciding what to wear,' he said drily. Lara tittered and one or two others also chortled their amusement. 'I'm going to skip the usual formalities. I beg your indulgence for this breach of protocol, but I'm going to hand the whole proceedings over to Q'zar, since it was he, and he alone, who demanded that we hold this extraordinary session at such short notice and at such an inconvenient time. Q'zar.' So saying, Darvin slumped back into his chair with a little less control than he would have liked.

'Fellow committee members, I have in my hands a report from forensics. It is of the gravest import and I believe you will all share my concerns on hearing its content. Approximately thirty-six hours ago an arm was discovered among the reeds of the lake in Happiland Park. A severed arm. This report states categorically that the arm belongs to a clone called Url. A clone has been murdered.' Q'zar watched them stir uncomfortably in their seats. He waited until the full significance of his words sank in before continuing: 'But that's not all. The report goes on to say that Url was murdered *at least* three days ago.'

Q'zar decided on the spur of the moment to convey more of the report to shake them out of their stupor. Only by hammering home the full horror of the crime, did he think he would get their permission to put into effect the drastic security measures he believed necessary.

Gorvik broke in: 'Why weren't we informed of this earlier. Presumably, he went missing? Why wasn't that reported?'

'Only Valchek can answer that question categorically, but as far as I am aware from an inspection of the Hub's record of work attendance, the clone was given permission to take a few days off because of influenza. We questioned the dormitory chief and he assumed he was in his room resting. When Valchek arrives,' Q'zar said with weary sarcasm, 'we shall find out if anything has gone unnoticed.'

'You said the report states about three days ago. Why isn't it more exact?' asked Sovran.

'The fact that the arm was partially submerged made it difficult to put an exact date on the crime,' replied Q'zar.

'Could it be possible the crime was committed the day prior to the banquet? When the arm was discovered by...' Arron's voice petered out.

'No, the report is clear that it was probably two or three days prior, and...' Q'zar looked up, turning toward the Chairman, '...Url was down for duty on the maintenance stairways on the night of the banquet. On that day, the dormitory chief reported that he could not be found.'

Darvin leaned forward with an expression of absolute incredulity. 'Do you mean to say that some clone, impersonating Url, possibly his murderer, was in the Tower on the night of the celebrations?'

'It looks like it,' answered Q'zar with equal distaste.

'It can't have been a clone,' Gorvik stated in his usual matter-of-fact tone. And before Q'zar could answer, he continued: 'Clone coding prevents them harming anyone.' He paused as he wondered if there was anything in this that could pose a threat to his proposals for reforming the Clone Laws. He then said, 'It's impossible.'

A silence fell upon the group as the bizarre nature of the crime began to register in their minds. Suddenly, Darvin, burst out angrily, 'Where is Valchek?' He picked up his telecom and barked an order for someone to go find him. He then looked back at Q'zar and, in a slightly more conciliatory tone, asked, 'Do you have any idea who the murderer is?'

'We're searching the entire city. All Watchers are on full alert. Of course, their number is few, but we will find the murderer.'

'Would that still apply if a clone began to deconstruct?' Sovran asked Gorvik. The story of Laia's shocking encounter with a deconstructed clone was still fresh in her mind. She was contemplating using it as the lead story for tomorrow's tablets. She had decided the time had come: she wanted to use the story to bring the whole issue of cloning into the open. But how, she rued, could she turn Laia's encounter into a pro-free clone campaign with a clonicide in the background?

Arron winced on hearing this question and began to think that all these events were conspiring against his wish to have Laia as his consort. Just before coming to the meeting, he'd had a furious argument with his secretary. He had learnt that she had not informed him of Laia's repeated efforts to contact him.

'You think that clone, one of our old models, the one you arrested, could have done this?' asked Darvin hopefully.

'No, I don't,' said Q'zar. 'But we must make it appear, for the meantime at least, that he is the culprit.' Q'zar turned to Sovran, holding up the report. 'You can't have a free hand on this. If the contents of go viral, we'll have a panic on our hands. That must be avoided at all costs.'

'It's a little premature to be demanding censorship, don't you think?' said Sovran, with a toss of her head. 'Every time there's some newsworthy event, you think NewsTalk and JT have to act as if it didn't exist. No, I don't agree. I think wild rumours are far more likely to create a panic than an informed article.' Inwardly, Sovran felt she had already crossed the Rubicon and was in no mood to kowtow to Q'zar's demands.

Arron would normally have sided with Q'zar on this issue, but, acutely aware that Laia was still under house arrest with a guard outside her door that even he could not get pass, he felt little inclined to do so. The sooner the news became public, the sooner Laia would be freed and the sooner the process of saving her reputation could begin.

'I can see the sense in that,' Arron acknowledged, nodding his approval in Sovran's direction and subsequently looking toward the Chairman for his agreement.

Darvin pulled himself up from the position he had slumped into. He seemed on the point of saying something, when he remembered that Valchek had still not turned up. He picked up his telecom and shouted to his secretary to go and find out what the blazes was keeping him so long. The secretary was unable to reply that someone had already been sent to find him before Darvin cut the line.

While Darvin was shouting into his telecom, a tap at the door had gone unheard. O entered. At first, no one recognized him. But as he walked toward his chair, memories were jogged and images of the man who had turned his back on politics and privilege began to re-assemble.

Q'zar was astounded at the change in his appearance. He had lost so much weight that his jowls hung from his rosy cheeks like two bags. However, his mop of silvery grey hair was as unkempt as ever. His clothes were the sort that less well-off citizens wore and his jacket was even patched at the elbows. Q'zar had always thought him eccentric, but now he wondered if he wasn't half-mad. But, more to the point, why now, after so many years of avoiding public life, should he turn up?

'I'm sorry to be late,' O said, in a voice so refined that it conveyed to everyone the nobility of his line. Resting his hands on the back of his chair, he looked along the table and said, 'I bear the saddest of news and I should not have troubled you with this unexpected appearance had it not been of the utmost seriousness. Valchek has been murdered in his apartment.'

A gasp reverberated around the room. For a moment, no one spoke and then everyone did except Darvin who sat mouth agog. Q'zar was ashen-faced. He felt stunned. A noble murdered in his penthouse suite!

O continued softly: 'There is something among us, something not human. On the night of the banquet, I was walking to my old apartment on the Topround to fetch a book. My eyes have grown weak and it was not brightly lit at the time, but as I walked I thought I saw a clone walking behind a director. I couldn't be sure who the director was because of his extraordinary attire. But now I feel sure it must have been Valchek and that the clone, if it was a clone, is the thing that is among us.'

'Why didn't you report this?' asked Darvin, lowering his head as if he were addressing a child.

'I did.'

Q'zar stirred uneasily. 'Probably hasn't been processed yet. Everyone was assigned to the celebrations.'

O continued: 'I decided to stay overnight. I was about to leave this morning when I heard a scream. I stepped out into the corridor and seeing Valchek's door open, I went to see what the matter was. A secretary lay on the floor. She must have fainted. As I leaned over and helped the woman to her feet, I saw Valchek's headless body. He has been decaptitated.' He paused and took a deep breath before continuing in a silence that a pin could have been heard to drop. 'The thing we seek is neither clone nor human. It's possible it has come from the Outside and has returned there. But if it is still among us, we are in danger. It has penetrated the innermost sanctuary of Joypolis.'

Every member of the committee sat riveted as O said, 'Q'zar, put guards at all the elevators and stairways. Limit all clones to their work area and living quarters. If the thing is among them, it must not enter the Tower.'

Q'zar responded by rattling off the list of measures he had prepared. He realized that all eyes were upon him now. He knew he needed to calm their fears by reassuring them that Joypolis was safe.

Gradually, an atmosphere closer to normality returned as questions were asked. Q'zar's request for more personnel to man the watching devices was quickly granted. Everyone offered personnel from their departments without argument. It was one of those rare occasions when the camaraderie of the directors rose above the petty squabbles of committee politics.

Darvin sensed it might be the right moment to end the meeting. He thanked Q'zar for his foresight, welcomed O back and suggested that Security and personnel details could be sorted out informally between the various secretaries of respective departments. Finally, he pronounced the meeting formally closed.

THE MARCH

It was early morning and mist still clung to the forest floor. In the glimmering, wet stillness several robots stood around the edge of a pit. One of their troop lay at the bottom but could not be seen. The leader of the troop, a humanoid called Sapor, ordered them to stand back. After they had moved back three paces, it sent a report of the incident to a distant headquarters.

The message ran:

- pit covered with sticks - sticks with leaves - colour identical to ground - 101 did not detect pit – has steep sides and mist prevents analysis - 101 in water at bottom - should rescue be attempted? -

After a few minutes, an incoming message made the photocells of its eyes glow red. Decoded, the message ran:

- state depth of pit and water -

Sapor encoded a reply:

- pit edge to water surface approximately one metre - depth of water not clear - analysis of stone drop test not clear - echo variability interference due to mud muffling stone contact with floor -

- can 101 stand? -

- 101 fell face down - no movement - does not respond to orders - likely reason short-circuiting due to water penetration -

- report position -

- coordinates g12 e38 - in grey section of forest - approximately 50 kilometres from destination -

- grey? - specify -

- trees covered with creeper - too high to obtain sample for analysis - creeper glistens in sun's rays - forms canopy that excludes 28

The reply was immediate: - proceed with march - do not attempt rescue - record position for possible rescue at future date - move out of grey area into open green space - new coordinates for your march will be relayed - proceed -

Sapor ordered the troop to get into line before standing at the head and leading their march.

As they climbed, they moved out of the Greylands into a greener and brighter part of the forest. Their metal casing absorbed the sun's heat into solar cells enabling them to draw less energy from their microfusion power packs. Not thinking to veer from the straight line of their course unless it was unavoidable, they slashed at everything that barred their way, leaving a swathe of destruction behind. Apart from the snapping and tearing of branches and the thud of their metallic feet, the only other sounds that could be heard were the shrieks of startled birds.

When Sapor received an incoming message, it ordered the troop to halt.

The message stated:

- 808 has accomplished its mission - it has murdered a director and left Joypolis - here are new coordinates for rendezvous - g34 e87 – estimated time three days - affirm coordinates -

Sapor executed a series of bleeps and received the final command:

- proceed to conquer Joypolis -

***

Moran moved away from the giant screen on which he could see the same view as Sapor. Previously, the screen had been a sandstorm of interference. This had been one reason for ordering them out of the Greylands, the other the lack of sunlight. He had chosen the route because it was the most direct and was curious to know why that part of the forest had turned grey, if, in fact, it had. Perhaps it had always been grey. There was so much out there that was unknown. But now, a wealth of information was being relayed to his computers by 808 and Sapor. Its analysis would take time, but, far more important was the fact that they were finally on their way to Joypolis. Only three more days, he thought clenching his bony right hand into a fist.

He had not forgotten how his ancestors had been forced out of the city to perish. Well, they hadn't. But they had suffered long enough. Soon, he thought, justice will be meted out. The citizens will obey or die, he swore.

He knew from 808's reports how meagre their defences were. How they wined, dined and played their time away. But he could not see the city itself. 808 was incapable of relaying visual messages from such a distance. Only Sapor could do that.

Moran shuffled toward the window that faced south. In the distance and far below, he could see forest and only forest. It spread for thousands of kilometres in all directions as far as the eye could see. But it was in that forest and far to the west that they had at last found Joypolis. The window at the opposite end of the room faced north and today, like so many others, a north-easterly was howling down the bleak valley it overlooked.

As Moran gazed out over the forest he recalled the valiant struggle of his forbears. How they had sought high ground so that they could know where there were in relation to Joypolis. They found none and became hopelessly lost as they travelled ever deeper into the forest. After months of wandering, they realized they were climbing and entering a different terrain. When they reached the saddle that linked these two peaks, they used the limestone caves they found here as shelters. While living in the caves, they sought a better place but found none. They decided to improve the caves by tunnelling deeper, linking passages and creating wider chambers. This done, they began to expand outward by using the plentiful supply of stones to build walls, courtyards, and outhouses. It was a heroic struggle. Yet the challenge of surviving in this inhospitable terrain, coupled with Koron III's single-minded desire for revenge, called forth a strength of purpose that epitomised the human spirit in adversity.

As the years passed, Koron realized his dream would not be fulfilled in his lifetime. To assure its completion, he created a battle plan that would span the generations. His task was to improve their shelter and make sure that the most capable trained the young in hunting and husbandry to guarantee a steady supply of food. Everything was used and nothing wasted. It was a harsh regime in which quarrels often broke out. The culprits were flogged till all obeyed his iron rule. The only respite from work were on those days set aside for ceremonies to re-enact the injustices they had suffered. In this way, no one would ever forget why they must seek revenge.

His successor, Koron IV, inherited a well-provided settlement. It was named East Peak since this peak was the first to be developed. His fort was perched on the highest point of the saddle that linked the peaks and guarded the dwellings within the caves beneath. During his life, the atmosphere began to change. Life was not always a struggle – there was time for relaxation. A steady supply of meat, grain and vegetables led to an increase in their number. However, there were occasions when hunters were lost. The cause was unknown, but when this happened, it reminded everyone of the forest's dangers.

The power source was electricity and it was generated by both water and windmills set within tunnels so the supply could be regulated. Eventually, this enabled them to set up the computer components that Koron had smuggled out of Joypolis. During Koron V's lifetime, they managed to run the systems used for programming basic robot parts. But it was not until Moran's reign that the rare metals needed to upgrade them were discovered at the base of the mountain. The first robots to be developed were only capable of lifting and carrying goods, but the breakthrough came years later with the creation of humanoids 808 and Sapor. With their production, Moran knew he had two robots that could lead a small force to attack Joypolis. But where was Joypolis?

Moran was in his sixties and beginning to despair that he would ever see the fabled city when a hunting party happened upon three savages. They questioned them as to where they had come from. They did not speak the same language but answered by gesture. They drew a tower they had passed. After putting them to the sword, the leader hurried back to tell Moran the most important piece of news to reach East Peak in over a hundred years. Joypolis lay to the north-west.

With this information, Moran was able to instruct 808 to find Joypolis. It had taken months, but, by eliminating errors, Moran was now able to plot a direct route that would take six weeks. Before 808 infiltrated Joypolis, Moran had Sapor and his troop set up antennae in trees along the new route to act as relay posts for communications. Once this was done, he ordered 808 to enter Joypolis and destabilize it with acts of terror.

808 began by observing the precincts nearest to the perimeter. When it entered at night, it discovered these districts were occupied by clones. Eavesdropping beneath a dormitory window, it heard that a clone named Url was ill and would not be able to work on the evening of the banquet. The dormitory chief asked who could cover his duties on the maintenance stairs. Seeing an opportunity to gain access to the upper floors of the Tower, 808 entered the dormitory during the night and murdered Url. Before disposing of his body in a lake, it removed his uniform and ID cards. It then scanned his face and modelled its features to a syntheskin mask that it used to cover its own. It entered the Tower on the night of the ball and carried out its next instruction – to kill a high-ranking director. After this, it left the city.

'The city shall be mine,' swore Moran. Turning away from the faint reflection in the window of his gaunt, hollowed-out features, he pulled his cloak more tightly around him. 'Once taken, the clones shall be slaughtered, slain like cattle.' He looked away from the clouds that obscured the West Peak and back at the screen on which he longed to see images of Joypolis. 'Only three more days,' he intoned ecstatically.

Man Ord

Once Ord reached the safety of the forest, he stopped running. He had to. It was too dark to see. The laser show had finished and the only light was a faint glimmer from the last road sign. He felt his way around bushes, the length and breadth of which he could only guess. Arms outstretched, he came to what he thought must be a massive tree. Feeling two knobbly roots at its base, he sat between them. Looking up, he could not see a single star but thanked them before falling into an exhausted sleep.

He had not slept long when drops of rain began to smack the back of his neck. He pulled at his collar, without lifting his head or changing his position. But when the rain began to splat harder, he stirred. Slipping his rucksack off, he stuffed its contents into his pockets and hauled it up over his head. In this way, he was able to catch snatches of sleep despite the downpour.

When he awoke, he found himself lodged uncomfortably between the exposed roots of a cedar tree. He was so stiff he could hardly move. Pushing himself up onto one of the roots, he began to rub life back into his legs. As he rubbed his calves and thumped his arms and shoulders to warm up, he looked around. Seeing his rucksack lying in a puddle, he picked it up and placed it on top of the other root. Pools of water were everywhere. The sun had risen but could not be seen for mist. Painfully, he stretched a leg out and felt how wet his trousers were. He wondered how long it would take them to dry.

When he stood up, he felt the weight of the things he had stuffed into his pockets. He knew that some of it was food. He pulled a bar of black chocolate out of his jerkin, tore the wrapping off and shoved pieces into his mouth. The relief he felt was immediate. He closed his eyes as he felt the chocolate melt and slide down his throat. He imagined his innards craning upward to receive this bitter-sweet river.

After he had eaten all the chocolate, he thought the mist had got thicker. Shelter, food, clothing, he told himself. It is not going to be easy, he thought, blowing into his hands. Hobbling out from under the tree, he decided to circle the city. He looked up at the tree he'd sheltered under. It was huge. A giant of the forest, he thought as he squelched through the puddles to get back to where the forest edged the perimeter.

As Ord picked his way in a clockwise direction around the city, he noticed the debris the downpour had left upon the forest floor. There were all sorts of birds foraging. Some were big and waddled, while others were scarcely bigger than his thumb. He grew warmer as he moved, but wished the sun would hurry up and get hotter as his trousers still stuck to his legs. He took another packet from his pocket. This time it was dried fruit. He began to eat them one by one. He wondered how he was going to survive. If every night was as cold as the last, he would need to build a shelter and make a fire. He wondered how he could do that without smoke revealing his whereabouts.

Preoccupied with these thoughts, he hardly noticed he was climbing. He was approaching the top of a small incline when he saw a deer appear below from out of the mist. He watched it munching the leaves of a bush. When it raised its head, pricked its ears and sniffed at the air, he saw how sensitively it was tuned to its surroundings. He then spotted another, probably its companion, on higher ground. As it stepped onto the ridge, it sent a shower of tiny stones tinkling down. In the same instant, there was a flash of light as if the sun had pierced the mist for a split second. He noticed the deer below bolt and vanish. Then, looking up, he saw the other lay on its side. A wisp of smoke curled from its flank.

Mystified, Ord stood staring at it. The stillness seemed to vibrate. He waited. When nothing happened, he decided not to carry on up to the top. Carefully, he stepped over some twigs to reach a rock. Crouching behind it, he recalled how the deer had fallen before the stones it had dislodged had even come to rest. He decided it would be safer not to move until the mist cleared.

When the mist lifted, he got up and peered through a gap between the two large rocks. Seeing nothing, he was about to carry on when a movement at the top of the ridge made him freeze. He could hardly believe his eyes. Could it be Url? He watched as Url tore his jacket off. He then ripped his trousers off. Seeing metal catch and reflect in the sunlight, Ord eased himself back. This was not Url. It was a robot. He looked again. It was tearing at its face, pulling rubbery strips off it. Stunned, Ord gulped back his fear. Instinct told him to run, but he remained still. The memory of the deer was still fresh in his mind.

808 inspected the deer it had killed before clumping away to rendezvous with the others.

Ord waited until its whirring sound could no longer be heard before getting up. He noticed his hands were shaking, but he decided to continue in the same direction to find the glade where he had discovered the tree with the face on it. He hoped to make a shelter there near the stream. As he walked on, he found it hard to shake off the grisly sight he had just witnessed. He stopped several times to try to make sense of it. What was a robot doing here? Why was it dressed as a Packer? And why did its face resemble Url's? He could make no sense of it, but took comfort from the fact that his clothes had dried. Loosening his collar, he pressed on.

THE CALM

As Ord journeyed toward the glade, the Emergency Meeting was breaking up. Everyone was reeling with shock at the news of Valchek's murder. Darvin was as white as a sheet and his eyes had taken on a woebegone look. O and Arron were trying to assure him that everything would be alright and there was no need to worry. Q'zar was explaining to Gorvik how they planned to ensure the Tower was safe before combing the city for the murderer. Sovran was trying to comfort Lara who was dabbing her cheeks with a handkerchief. As she did so, she kept shooting glances in the direction of Q'zar. She needed to speak to him. She guided Lara to the door and asked a secretary to see her back to her apartment. As she turned back, she nodded to Gorvik who was on the way out. She went and joined the others who were listening to Q'zar.

'We'll start from the top and work down. We have to be absolutely sure the thing is not inside. We'll search every square centimetre. I'll need more personnel. Arron, Sovran can either of you help? Gorvik's promised fifty today and a hundred tomorrow.'

'Yes, of course,' replied Arron. 'I can let you have thirty immediately. But for Code's sake, don't have them searching people's rooms! Get them to search the utility rooms of each floor... But what am I going to tell them?'

'Tell them it's only a temporary duty, a 'special task' and they'll be back at their desks soon enough. We don't want rumours flying around about a beast on the loose. It'd cause a panic. But I'm going to need more than that. Could you let me have double that number and more tomorrow if we haven't found it?'

'I'll do my best,' said Arron. 'Look, why don't we get the entire population involved? Get something out on the news, Sovran. Not the truth, of course. But say a child has been lost, pluck everybody's heartstrings, get News Talk to appeal for everyone's help – even the clones – to search everywhere. But don't forget to add that if they do come across anything unusual to report it immediately.'

'No problem. Leave it to me. I may change the line. Jewels might be better. Oh, and I'll need to interview Laia Drovny. Can you let the guard know? I'll do that first. Then I'll send some people over to your section.'

'Thank you,' replied Q'zar, wondering why in the Codes, Sovran wanted to interview Drovny. He was on the point of asking, but checked himself. If he denied her access, she would refuse him personnel. 'I'll inform the guard, but be careful what you write. We need to contain this. If we don't, we'll be involved in a damage limitation exercise and that's the last thing we need.'

'You can rely on me,' Sovran lied.

'Now, about personnel, how many can you spare...?' Q'zar asked Sovran.

As Q'zar and Sovran continued to talk, O had drawn Darvin to one side. Standing together in profile, they looked rather similar. Neither was tall and both plump. But in dress, they could not have been more dissimilar.

Darvin was wearing a formal suit and O a light tweed jacket with brown corduroy trousers.

'Of course, it must be a state funeral,' O was saying. 'Sad, very sad business. My father knew his father very well. Often spoke of him with the greatest admiration.'

'We've lost a brave man today,' said Darvin, feeling his stomach ache with all the food and drink he'd consumed at the banquet. 'Worse thing to happen in Joypolis for a long, long time. Never anything like this. A noble!' he groaned.

O laid a comforting hand on Darvin's arm. 'Don't you worry. Q'zar'll get to the bottom of this. Once we know what it is and where it's hiding, we'll kill it or drive it back to the wild,' he said, trying to rally Darvin's spirits. 'Something you could think about is who is going to replace him. And, oh yes, what about the funeral? Who's going to sort out the details?'

These practical questions helped to focus Darvin's mind. 'Yes, yes, of course, the funeral. I'll speak to Zuriko about that. She's rather good at that sort of thing, you know. A lot of the things you saw at the banquet were her doing. She's a dab hand at that sort of thing. And yet, so modest. Never expects any credit for what she does.' A thought suddenly made Darvin's blood run cold. 'Thank the Founders it wasn't her,' he gasped. 'But, don't misunderstand me, I'm not suggesting...'

'Of course not,' O replied reassuringly and, taking him by the elbow, guided him toward the door. He continued to nod his head as Darvin went on about possible replacements and how, once Zuriko had put forward some ideas for the funeral, it would be necessary to call a meeting to sort out details. O even promised to attend the meeting as Darvin told him how much they had all missed him and demanded to know where he had been hiding.

After reaching an agreement on the number of personnel she could release, Sovran decided to leave since Arron seemed impatient to talk to Q'zar in private.

'Well, that's about all for the moment. Thank you, Arron. You've been a great help. I must go, but I'll keep you informed.'

'Just a moment,' said Arron, placing a hand on Q'zar's forearm. 'What about Laia Drovny? I mean, surely you can release her from house arrest? Even I can't get past that confounded guard you've stuck outside her door!'

'I'm sorry. But believe me, when this wretched business is over, I'll not only lift the order for her house arrest, I will personally commend her for bravery and nominate her for the Exceptional Citizen's Award. Please understand,' said Q'zar, squeezing his arm in a gesture of camaraderie, 'security must come first. If she said as much as one word about this to anyone, we'd have mayhem on our hands. And,' Q'zar said, raising a hand to silence Arron's objection, 'don't forget, if they start clamouring for the facts, it will, as you well know, unsettle the clones. I don't have to tell you of all people, clone conditioning only works against a controlled background and it's the citizens that act as tokens of that background. Gorvik will tell you the same. We can't risk it.' Seeing Arron's crestfallen expression, Q'zar added, 'But I give you my solemn word that when this is over, she'll be hailed as a heroine.'

'All right,' Arron sighed reluctantly. 'But, please, at the earliest possible moment, and not a jot later, lift this odious order.'

'I will,' Q'zar replied squarely. 'Now, Arron, I must go. Please let me have those extra hands as soon as possible.'

'I'll see to it now,' Arron replied, despondently.

***

Zuriko snapped her telecom shut. Darvin had told her everything. Murdered, O says... O! Where did he suddenly pop up from? O thinks it's not human, but something from the Outside. Watchers combing the city. Q'zar says they'll find it by dawn. Ideas for a funeral. Great Codes! She closed her eyes.

She remained like this for a few moments, letting it sink in. Then, getting up from the sofa, she walked to the window and looked down. It was quiet. After the banquet few would be out and about. Most would be at home recounting, time and again, the excitement and beauty of that night. Nothing seemed different. Yet, somewhere, she thought with morbid fascination, a murderer is hiding or even walking about, his chest stuck out, cocksure he's covered his tracks... Stalking his next victim even.

Recently, she had been thinking a lot about murder. Soon, it must be soon, she thought. Perhaps, he, it, whatever, is driven by the same voices as me. Closing her eyes, she began to sway slightly. She let herself slip-slide down inside, deeper and deeper, until she felt as distant as a tiny star. She listened to her breathing sigh like tiny waves upon an unseen shore. Purple shapes floated through orange light until an image of herself hunched over an egg appeared. Her forehead clunked against the glass of the window. The egg cracked and oily fluid poured out. A blade-like fin shone as it cut its way through the smooth black surface. Her eyes opened. 'A knife,' she murmured. 'But when?' she asked.

She went and poured herself a drink. After sipping it, she flipped her telecom open.

'Is that you, Warton?'

'What's up?' he said, recognizing her voice.

'All right to speak now, is it?'

'Better be quick. We're up to our ears.'

'Oh, I know. Valchek murdered! And on the night of the ball! Awful!'

The silence that followed told her that Warton had not been informed.

'Look, we're real busy, I'm going to have to ring off...' Warton said, taken aback.

'No, listen. I wanted to tell you about that girl. You know, the one you said you wanted. Laia Drovny's her name...'

'What about her?'

'Well, now's your chance. She's under house arrest, you know that of course, but I hear they're going to release her soon. I'll arrange a time for you.' Breaking the silence, Zuriko teased, 'You don't want to miss out, now do you?'

'Okay,' Warton replied, his eyes narrowing.

The Headline

After speaking to Q'zar, Sovran went straight to Laia's room. As she hurried along the Midround corridor, she felt this was the moment – the opportunity to blow the whole clone issue wide open. Thinking she had better warn Gorvik, she called him and explained what she was going to do.

'Do it,' he said simply but emphatically.

'I just need the angle,' Sovran said. 'This woman may have it. I want to know about the clone she met. He crossed to the Outside several times. Gotta ring off,' she said as the guard posted at Laia's door came into view.

She produced her ID. It had already been cleared by Q'zar, but the guard checked it before pushing a button on the door.

Laia opened the door and looked up at Sovran. Surprised, she took a step back.

'Sovran Dellovar. May I come in?'

Laia knew who she was. Sovran was a celebrity. 'Yes, of course.' Laia stepped aside, wondering what in the Codes she owed this visit to.

'I'm sorry you're still not allowed to leave,' Sovran said. 'It's Q'zar, you know. If there's one thing he hates, it's the truth. He doesn't want anybody to hear about that arm you found until he's got the culprit behind bars.'

'I missed the banquet because of it.' Laia said, dejection written all over her face.

'I'm sorry. But the reason I came to see you is not about the arm. It's about the clone you met. Could you tell me about him, Laia?'

'Eh?' Laia frowned. Puzzled, she asked, 'Tell you what?'

'Everything. Everything.' Sovran said, staring straight into Laia's eyes.

'Well,' Laia said, gesturing Sovran to sit on the sofa as she took the chair opposite. 'I was told he was a Carer once. The last of his kind. He was called Ord after the coding of his batch. Awful name, don't you think? Anyway, he was transferred into the Hub as they were short of Packers and because of that he began deconstructing earlier than usual. But he'd gone to the...' She gestured toward the perimeter. 'Not once, but a lot. Zuriko begged me to find out what he'd done and seen out there. She kept on and on until I finally gave in and agreed.

'Yes. Zuriko, my so-called soul sister, contacted me because only I, she said, could wheedle the information out of him.' She rolled her eyes. 'The Chairman himself would hear of my good work, she promised. This was a special assignment.' Laia cast her eyes upward, 'What a fool I was! She did it deliberately. I just know it. She wanted to ruin my reputation and probably has.'

'You could've refused,' Sovran said, puzzled at the bitterness in Laia's voice.

'Yes, and I wish I had. But... I trust people too easily.'

'Did the clone get nasty?' Sovran asked, trying to bring the conversation back to what she was interested in.

'No, not really. But the whole thing has made me a pariah, hasn't it? That's why, all of a sudden, I was off the guest list for the banquet.' Laia looked so tearful that Sovran took her keen gaze off her for a few moments to rummage a tablet out of her shoulder bag.

'So you think you were left off the guest list because you agreed to meet this clone?' Sovran asked, looking back and setting the tablet to record.

'Yes. Well, you tell me. I don't know.' Laia got up and walked across to the window. 'All I know is that I'm under house arrest for doing what a citizen is supposed to do – report anything out of the ordinary. After, not before I met that clone, a rumour started going around that he was... unclean, that he'd contracted some disease from meeting barbarians... I don't believe it. It was malicious rumour. And whoever started it, started it deliberately, knowing full well whose reputation was at stake. I believe Zuriko was behind it.'

'When I get out of here, I'm going to tell her what I think of her and... and ... Oh, when are they going to take that guard off my door! I'm sick of this! I can't contact anyone! I can't even receive calls! How much longer is this going to go on for?'

'Don't worry. Trust me. When this story hits the streets it'll create such a storm that Q'zar won't know what's hit him. There'll be no point in keeping you cooped up in here any longer. Believe me. The whole thing'll be out in the open where it should've been right from the start.'

Laia returned to her seat. She was thinking there's something about this Dellovar woman. The way she speaks makes you believe her. Feeling the intensity of Sovran's gaze, Laia sensed she was going to do something important. It made her feel better, more hopeful. But what was she going to write?

'Why don't you do something on Zuriko? They say she's rolling in money and a lot of it's not legal.'

'She is, as you say, very powerful and wealthy. But Laia, believe me, you'll be out tomorrow and you'll be able to get back to normal life.'

Laia smiled, 'I hope so. I really do.'

'Now, tell me more about the clone. The clone. Was he violent?'

'No. I was scared, but no, he wasn't violent. I would call it desperate, lonely, driven to despair. Like me!' she said with an ironic humph. Then, continuing, 'No, he was gentle. That's what they're supposed to be, isn't it? Carers are, aren't they?'

Sovran nodded as Laia carried on: 'He told me he'd seen me before. On the day he submitted a C80. That seemed to upset him.'

When Laia finished telling her story, Sovran said, 'Hmm, we're told that they can't feel love or any deep emotion, but I'm beginning to wonder after what you've just said if that's true. Sounds as if this clone was in deep distress and feeling just as much hurt as we do. If they're more like us than we've been led to believe, then what does that make us?' Sovran asked herself more than Laia.

'I don't get you... Are you saying we're the same?'

'Well, think about it. The picture you've given me is of a clone, an ex-Carer, driven to despair by abandonment. So, what does he do? He's so desperate he heads for there.' Sovran nodded Outward. 'And you tell me he was crying for help before he was dragged out of your room by that horrible Watchman.' Laia nodded. 'So, what does this make us? We may not be personally involved in cracking the whip above their heads, but look what happens when they deconstruct.' Sovran splayed her hand like a fan toward Laia. 'They're bussed to the Encrypt and disposed of like some kind of consumable. And what do we do? Nothing. So, tacitly, we condone it.'

Laia looked down and in a very quiet voice, asked, 'Do you really believe this?'

'Gorvik says their presence undermines the initiative of the manager classes. Undermine! I think he's got his priorities the wrong way around. If this clone is in need of care and kindness, how can we do this to him? How can *we* be so inhuman?'

'But...' Laia didn't know what to say.

'They all die earlier than we do 'cos they're cloned from clones, but some – and the clone you saw is one of them – are transferred out of jobs they were trained to do. These are the ones that get junked for anti-social behaviour. There aren't many. But all of them are eventually disposed of when they're no longer able to work. And we all accept the official line that they are LPRs, half-wits, quarter brains, who don't feel like we do. So, what's this clone doing, crying out for help! He needs help – love and tender care is what he needs!' Sovran slipped her tablet back into her case and stood up. 'Thank you. I've got to go Laia.'

'Oh, right. Yes.' Laia got up and walked with her to the door.

Seeing the look of despair return to Laia's face, Sovran took her hand and gave it a gentle squeeze. 'Don't worry. Tomorrow, you'll be out. I promise.'

'I hope so'. She smiled sadly. 'I really can't stand this much longer.'

'Incredibly, there's a rumour going around that the clone escaped from the Encrypt,' Sovran said as she twirled her fingers bye-bye to Laia with a final, 'Cheer up.'

When the door closed, Laia suddenly felt more alone than before. She walked to the window. In the distance, she could see Happiland Park. If Sovran could visit her, she wondered why Arron couldn't.

Sovran almost ran back to her offices. She had the angle, she felt the rush. Words were pouring into her head. The headline: *Who will care for the clones?* 'Tomorrow,' she swore, 'I'll change this city forever. To hell with Q'zar!'

O

O had pored over the documents he had taken from Valchek's apartment late into the night. When voices outside his window pricked his consciousness, he realized he must have fallen asleep in his armchair. Some papers lay on his lap while others had slid off onto the floor. He winced at the crick in his neck, and, as he pulled himself up, more papers sailed down to join the rest.

One paper caught his attention. On it was the sign that Valchek must have been investigating. O knew it only too well. It was Koron's seal. Of that there could be no doubt. Cranking himself up into a sitting position, he told himself it had nothing to do with Valchek's murder. A mere coincidence. Why then, he asked himself, do I have this horrible feeling?

O pushed his arms down hard to propel himself upward. As he wobbled out of control toward the sink, he thought if the thing is not an animal, but a robot, then what? Koron? After all these years? Surely not! Steadying himself, he stared into the sink. Distracted by the kerfuffle outside, he went to close the window. As he struggled to shut it, he could see several neighbours arguing in the alley below. One of them was stabbing a finger at a tablet. O caught snatches: 'course we're not like them...' and 'why shouldn't we be allowed to clone our own?' and 'have real people cloned like Gorvik says here...'

O shut the window and stepped back. Running a hand through his directionless mop of white hair, he murmured, 'Oh Codes no, not now, not now. This is the last thing we need. Please Sovran, not the Clone Laws, not now of all times, please.' His shoulders sagged as he tottered back to the sink and fished out a cup of unfinished black coffee. Grimacing, he sipped on it. 'I'd better go see Q'zar,' he thought, uttering a heartfelt yuck at the coffee's foul taste. He pulled his coat on and left by a rickety staircase that led down to the alley in which his neighbours were still haranguing one another.

O lived in Joypolis' poorest and most notorious district – the Maze. It was aptly named as visitors quickly became lost in its labyrinthine streets. O knew it like the back of his hand and was soon stepping out of one of its narrow lanes into the cleaner air of Dovan Square. As he crossed the square heading toward a public walkway, he paused to look up at the monument of his most famous forbear – Dovan V. He would have told his son, the same as my father told me, he thought. Of that, he was sure. He would never forget the dreaded tones in which his father spoke of Koron III: 'A formidable enemy and an even deadlier friend,' he had said when he explained why the Andradists had been driven out of the city and why this story had to be handed down from generation to generation to keep alive the danger that he believed Koron's descendants could still pose if they survived and attempted to return.

O recalled how his father described Koron as an evil genius. At first, he had not been opposed to cloning. But this was because he wanted to conduct experiments on them to learn more about the human brain and develop the type of advanced micro-circuitry needed for humanoids. The ruling faction flatly refused to condone such research, describing it as inhuman. Dovan feared that if such machines were developed, they would not be used for the common good but to seize power from the state. He was right. When one of Koron's scientists blew the whistle on his research, it became clear that they were using clones and were on the brink of an important breakthrough. Dovan knew that if they did not act quickly, they would be at the wrong end of a coup d'état.

Koron's rage at his betrayal and banishment struck terror into all who witnessed it. The vengeance he swore he would wreak upon the city and the curses he invoked upon the heads of those who ordered them out on pain of death left no one unmarked. They did not attempt to return, but the discovery of an underground passage that looked as if it had been used to smuggle out valuable robot parts and computer systems made them wary. But as the years passed, the threat faded into the background and was all but forgotten.

Stepping onto a walkway, O could not fail to notice the buzz of excitement. Commuters who had never spoken to one another were now lifting their tablets and commenting on Sovran's articles. One person was saying, 'Maybe this *is* the answer, if a clone can go Out there and come back, well, maybe we can expand.' Then another, 'We all thought it was dangerous, but if he came back and was alright...'

He snatched a printed copy of *The Joypolitan* as he passed a stack. His head began to reel on reading it. His first thought was that Q'zar must be fuming. The headline read: 'Jewels in the City'. It continued with an appeal to readers to report anything unusual, but then went on to pose the question: 'Who will care for the clones? Who will search their districts? Few citizens will bother to enter their districts. Of course, the clones will also be told to search and report anything unusual. But will they search as carefully? Of course not, they've not been conditioned for this. They can only do one job well. But that's not the end of it. This is just one weakness of a segregated society. How much longer can we tolerate this situation?'

A further headline announced: '*Joypolitan* says it's time for change!' This column was unequivocally about reforming the Clone Laws. Darvin as well as Q'zar must be calling for her blood, thought O. There was even a contribution from Gorvik headed: 'Real Clones From Real People', stating that machines could do their menial tasks and that only when they started cloning for intelligence could the city move forward in the way that the Founders advocated. Articles on resurrection cloning followed, including the right to have a genetic copy of a loved one who died prematurely. It was endless. The entire edition was given over to the issue of Joypolis' future. There was a questionnaire for readers to fill in and submit regarding the type of society they wanted, whether to expand Outward and how best to set up a public debate.

O could feel the prickly energy coming off the crowd around him. Unable to bear it any longer, he stepped off at a junction and, on an impulse, stepped onto another walkway that was far less crowded. I need space, he thought, as he once more turned his attention to the articles and the controversy they had whipped up.

Surprised at reaching a terminal, he stepped off and walked down to the street. He was wondering why it was so quiet when it dawned on him that he must have taken the wrong walkway. He had gone in the opposite direction to the Tower and ended up on the outskirts. Shoving the paper into his pocket, he muttered 'fool' under his breath. He knew his head was often in the clouds, but this really was too much. He told himself to keep his mind on the Outside.

His head jerked at this slip of the tongue. He looked down the street. He could see it led to the perimeter. How odd, he thought, quietly repeating what he'd said: 'Keep my mind on the Outside. Reality is what I meant to say, but here I am almost on the Outside!' On an impulse, he began to walk toward the perimeter. He knew the security cameras were filming him, but he did not care.

He stopped when the road ended. How odd, he thought. I've never seen the end of a road before. Looking down at his scuffed shoes sticking over the edge, he felt a rush of light. What is it, he wondered, closing his eyes trying to steady himself. When he opened them, everything was vibrating. An aura trembled at the edge of each object and in the air, he saw curls twist and untwist like maggots. He felt he was swirling in a vortex.

Raising both hands to the sides of his head, he whispered and then shouted, 'That's it! That's why! Inner-Outer! To the outer reality! The other side! One side defines the other! The lie needs the truth as the truth needs the lie! Eureka!'

He swung round several times, wondering if he should race back and tell them. But who would listen? Why, why didn't I see it before? What a fool I've been! We must go to the Outside to find ourselves, to create ourselves, to grow out of our blinkered existence...' Hearing something fall nearby, he scanned the ground around him. Seeing nothing, he was about to return to his thoughts when a movement at the perimeter caught his attention. He could see a man standing at the edge of the forest waving. O blinked. Was he imagining this?

As he watched, the man threw something. It fell a few paces from him. Still lost in what seemed to him the mountains of the mind muttering inner-outer, one entails the other, he went and picked it up. It was wrapped in paper. He recognized the paper – it was a ration chit of the sort clones used. He was on the point of stuffing it into his pocket when the man shouted, 'Robots!' O turned but he had gone.

With the word reverberating in his ears, O unravelled the paper and read what was scrawled on the back: 8 ROBOTS. He felt shock waves rock him from head to foot. He tore off up the street.

When he reached the walkway, he was completely out of breath and pulled himself up the stairs by the rail one at a time. His jowls shook with fear at the knowledge he now knew to be true: Koron was back.

***

Ord waited till O was out of sight. Good, he thought, now I can get what I came for – food. His stomach was empty and his nerves at breaking point. It had not been a good morning. On his way to scavenge the tips that bordered the perimeter, he had seen another robot – a whole troop of them. Hearing a dull mechanical noise, he hid himself and waited until the thud of metallic feet receded before parting the tall ferns. He saw them march into the same glade he had spent the night and meet the one he had seen the previous day. He counted eight. Ord watched them standing around a giant of their kind bleeping. He did not dare move. He had seen how they could kill from a distance. As he waited, he grew hungrier. When they finally pounded off in different directions, he headed for the tips.

On the way, he kept asking himself what are robots doing so close to Joypolis? He was mystified. When he reached the edge of the forest that faced the tips, he saw O. He did not expect to see anyone at the perimeter. He did not want to cross with someone watching. They would tell the Watchers and they would be waiting for him the next time he came. He hid behind a tree. But hunger forced his hand. He decided to throw something at the man. Tell him there were robots. See how he reacts. He certainly reacted. As soon as O turned tail and ran, Ord dashed across to the tip.

Climbing its lumpy slope, he ducked and weaved his way across the top, stopping to pick up things he thought useful. Every now and then, he stopped and craned his neck to make sure the coast was clear. It was, as he expected, deserted. But when he spotted an unmanned vehicle approaching, he almost jumped for joy. Yesterday's leftovers, he thought, as he raced to position himself closer to where it would dump its load.

***

By the time O reached the Topround, it was past midday. Breathless and clutching his heart, he hobbled toward Darvin's offices. As he approached, he was stopped by a Watchman who demanded to see his ID. O did not have it. He shoved O up against the wall and frisked him. Satisfied he was unarmed, he began questioning him.

'Name?'

'O,' came the gasped reply. 'Look, I've got to see Q'zar. It's important.'

'Oh what?'

'I've just told you, for Code's sake. I am O, Head of Belief, the sole living descendant of Dovan V. Now let me pass before I have you reported.'

The guard made a call. Without cutting the call, he looked back at O. 'What's the number of your residence,' he asked.

O rattled off his old address. The guard repeated it. 'He's a short guy, wearing a long overcoat. Yeah, white hair, yep, that fits. Okay.' Looking back at O, he said, 'Somebody'll be along in a minute.'

O threw his hands up and walked up and down, knowing he could do nothing. Finally, Hersh arrived and escorted him to Darvin's offices where the secretary put a call through to Darvin. After a couple of minutes, Darvin stuck his head around a door. 'Yes, that's him. Come in, old boy.'

Hersh stepped back and the secretary stood up as O shot forward and Darvin closed the door behind him.

'You really ought to carry some ID,' began Darvin, as they walked to his office at the far end. 'You couldn't have come at a worse time. You've seen the news, I suppose. What a mess! Every malcontent clamouring to be heard! There's a demonstration on the Midround! For free cloning! Can you believe it? And to top it all, Q'zar hasn't found the murderer. It's chaos!'

As they entered Darvin's office, they were confronted with a furious argument.

'Why is it, every time there's something interesting to report, you forbid it!' Sovran shouted, jabbing a finger at Q'zar.

'You've created a panic! With the citizens clamouring for explanations, the clones are getting restless! What in the Name of the Codes did you think you were doing!' Q'zar yelled back.

'There is no panic. What you see on the Midround is real people wanting to face reality, wanting to take their lives into their own hands. People who are sick and tired of the lies that you and other nobles believe you have the right to spoon-feed them.'

'How dare you!' exclaimed Q'zar, his pinched features drawn tight enough to split.

O pushed himself between them.

'Stop it, stop it, please,' he cried, raising his hands above his head. 'Look, look at this,' he said, holding up a scrap of paper. Both Sovran and Q'zar stared at it as O told them what had happened at the perimeter.

Q'zar snatched the paper from O. He knew it must have been thrown by the clone who had escaped, though he said nothing.

Finally, O whispered, 'Don't you see?' And then in an even deadlier whisper: 'Koron is back!' Pointing, he hissed, 'His robots are out there.'

A picture began to form in Q'zar's mind. The murderer was a robot. They had not found it because it had left the city. If the clone's message could be believed, there were eight. Valchek's murder was merely a foretaste of what was to come, an act of terror intended to distract and destabilize. He flipped his telecom open.

'Get me Warton,' he demanded, walking toward the window away from the group of three who stood facing one other each lost in their own private thoughts. Puzzled at there being no reply, Q'zar put a call through to Security HQ and asked them to contact him. Then, almost beside himself, he barked, 'What do you mean, you can't? Try again.'

While he waited, Q'zar said to the others, 'This changes everything. If this is true, we're no longer looking for a murderer. We're facing an attack on the city.' He looked over his shoulder. Clouds were darkening the sky. He flipped his telecom open again, 'Hersh? Listen carefully. I want all forces redeployed. Yes, all. It's red alert. Just listen, will you? Yes, I repeat it is red alert. Now, you know the procedure. Good. Lower ranks to guard the perimeter at the road junctions; second line of defence at the ring formed by Founders Square linking Happiland Broadway to Dovan's Place. That's right. The last line of defence is at the base of the Tower. We're facing an attack by eight robots. As soon as you contact Warton, put him through. Yes, I'll be with you as soon as I can. And I want you to remain in the Tower. That's right.'

He snapped his telecom shut and turned to Darvin. 'We'll use your offices as headquarters. Tell all directors and key personnel to come here and remain on the Topround. I'll have my men disperse the demonstration on the Midround. I've declared red alert and that means a curfew.' Then shooting daggers at Sovran, he yelled, 'Media blackout, got it?'

Sovran was about to let rip when O said: 'Look!'

The lights went out momentarily and then flickered back on as they turned toward the window where O stood pointing to a trail of light moving across the sky.

'A comet?' ventured O, as they all gave each other a look of mild surprise.

The Storm

Warton smirked at the sight. All along the Midround, citizens clamouring at the doors of officials, waving papers and banners and chanting, 'Referendum, referendum, referendum.' Perfect, he thought. His pace faltered when his telecom rang and he saw it was from Q'zar. To hell with it, he thought, tossing it into a refuse chute.

Outwardly, his face looked no different than normal. But inwardly he was flying high. All day he had been seething, but now he was up there, ready to let rip. He'd lost count of how many uppers he'd popped. Couple of tubes? He could feel heat burn across his shoulders. He could feel heat as he curled his fingers one by one into a fist and in the intent of each movement toward the fulfilment of his goal. It was party time.

He stepped off the main corridor just as the PA system blared a red alert. Warton stopped. The demonstrators fell silent. Everyone froze. Then someone shouted it was a hoax and the demonstrators began to protest even more loudly.

The guard at Laia's door stood to attention on seeing Warton approach.

'At ease,' Warton said, taking out a pack of cigarettes and offering him one.

'Thank you, Domo.'

'Anything to report?'

'Nothing, Domo.'

'Well, you can go now.'

'Go, but...?'

'It's okay. You're needed at the perimeter. Go to North Junction 8. Everything's changed. It's red alert. We've been told to defend the city.'

'It's probably a false alarm,' Warton said, seeing the guard's dumbfounded expression. 'They...' He thumbed toward the protesters, '...think it's a hoax. But you better get moving.'

As the guard made to go, Warton said, 'Oh, let me have your telecom, can't seem to find mine. You can get another one from Braun later.'

The guard unclipped his telecom and handed it over, stunned at the news and wondering at how Warton could be so flippant.

Warton turned the telecom over in his hand, waiting until the guard was out of sight before entering Laia's apartment.

***

On hearing of the red alert, Arron headed straight for Darvin's offices. By the time he arrived, it was pandemonium. Secretaries were carrying equipment out of one office into another, security personnel everywhere. Flashing his ID, Arron walked along the normally quiet corridors, squeezing to one side as a stream of secretaries bustled past.

He entered Darvin's outer office and stopped to take in the scene that met his eyes. Q'zar was shouting orders down his telecom, Sovran was in a corner covering one ear trying to hear a conversation on hers. O was seated, gazing at the floor while Lara paced up and down in front of him. In the adjoining room, he could see security personnel sat in front of an array of screens that had been assembled to view strategic points of the city.

'Where's Gorvik?' Arron asked, looking around and wondering if the world had gone mad.

'He says he'll be along shortly. Got to make sure his tissue banks are safe first,' Darvin answered, glancing nervously at the darkness outside.

'Can't he get someone else to do that?'

'Apparently not,' Darvin said irritably. His thoughts were elsewhere. He had been trying to contact Zuriko unsuccessfully for the last hour. He wanted her by his side.

'What in the Codes is going on?' Arron asked, directing his question at no one in particular.

Sovran, finishing her call, managed to answer before another call came: 'Q'zar thinks the city's going to be attacked. O says he saw robots on the Outside.'

'Robots!'

'No, no,' cried O. 'I didn't see them. A clone saw them. He scribbled a message that read eight robots and threw it at me.'

'Threw it at you?'

'Yes, we think a robot may have murdered Valchek,' said O, stirring in his chair but too tired to explain everything all over again.

Arron looked over at Q'zar who was still talking down his telecom. 'Look Hersh, have someone go down and let Chu out. Yes, that's right. We need every man we have and he's one of our best. Brief him on the situation.'

Arron looked around and was on the point of asking Darvin what he thought, when suddenly a flash of light lit the sky. As everyone turned toward the window, a dull boom was heard. They could see nothing, but someone from the adjoining room called out: 'It's the Old Bio. It's been hit!' From the window, they could see a large cloud of grey dust billow up. Before they could utter a word, someone in the other room called them to the screens. Q'zar rushed in followed by the others.

One screen showed a robot at North Gate, another one at the South-west Gate, and yet another could be seen appearing at the South Gate. Gradually, eight robots were visible as well as the irreparable damage their thin laser fire was inflicting. Seemingly oblivious to the gunfire of those defending the perimeter, they moved methodically forward. One screen flashed red: perimeter defence breached at north-east sector.

Arron's first thoughts were for Laia. He looked at Q'zar. 'Is Drovny still being held?'

At first, Q'zar didn't answer. His attention was riveted to the images of the robots.

Arron shook his shoulder. 'I said, is Laia Drovny still being held?'

'What? Yes, wait.' Q'zar turned to a sub-lieutenant and told him to call the guard at Laia's door.

'No answer, Domo.'

Q'zar looked at Arron and raised a hand in a gesture of utter bewilderment.

Arron rushed out of the room. Q'zar was about to rush after him, but, looking back at the screens, his feet turned to lead as he saw buildings near the first line of defence collapse and clones running and screaming in all directions. Just then, his telecom rang. He saw it was from Chu.

'Look's bad, Domo. May I respectfully suggest all key citizens be allowed to take refuge in the Midround?'

'Yes, give the order. And Chu, I... come up here. Finish what you're doing, then come up and, oh yes, there's one other thing, before you come...'

***

Laia lay on the sofa reading *News Talk* on her tablet. She was thinking Sovran really had stirred things up. She had nothing but praise for Laia 'volunteering to meet the clone.' She wondered at that choice of words. Still, what did it matter if she was free tomorrow. But what was the red alert about, she thought. Was it to disperse the demonstrators whose chanting she could still hear? Hearing the door open, she swung round.

She recognized the Watcher. He was the one who had brought Ord. She put the tablet down and got up.

'What do you want?' she asked coldly.

Warton did not answer. He looked around as if there was something he had come to find.

'I asked you a question. You don't just walk in here without knocking!'

Warton walked casually over to her.

'Get out!' Laia shouted, pointing at the door.

She did not see his eyes narrow, but she did sense something menacing in the way he worked his tongue over his front teeth.

Warton sighed, looked from side to side, ignoring her question with a kind of hang-dog expression, before he struck her hard across the face with the back of his hand.

Laia gasped as she reeled backward.

When she came to a stop, she was shaking. Warton rushed over and threw her on to floor. As she tried to get up, he kicked her hand away so that she fell face down onto the carpet. As soon as she rolled over, Warton sat on top of her and pushed her V-neck top up over her face.

Feeling his rough hand snap her bra free, she struck him as hard as she could on the side of his head with her elbow, then grabbed his ear and wrenched it so hard she managed to slip out from beneath him. But before she could stand up, he had grabbed her from behind and pulled her down again. Her screams were cut short by another hard slap across the face. Blood trickled out of the corner of her mouth. She twisted sideways to shield herself from more blows, but no sooner had she done so than she felt the slobber of his tongue on her neck.

Feeling her buttocks hard against him, Warton was well lusted up. He started to yank her slacks down with one hand while his right pulled her head back by the hair. She heard him grunt, 'It's no good screaming. Guard's gone, I'm here, now you can be good, bad, either way makes no difference...'

Suddenly, the door opened.

Warton leapt to his feet.

Arron took one look at Laia's terror-stricken face and realized immediately what had been going on. Laia covered her breasts as she rushed to his side in the doorway.

Up to this point, neither Warton nor Laia had noticed the distant rumbling of the battle at the perimeter. Arron walked up to Warton, his eyes blazing with fury.

'Get out!' he shouted, pointing toward the door with Laia cowering behind him.

As Warton straightened his tunic and made to brush himself down, he knew he had crossed the point of no return. It was all-or-nothing now. He walked to the door, drew his gun on his blind side, closed the door, turned and shot Arron in the back.

Laia jumped at the sound and, in the same instant, saw Arron collapse in a heap at her feet. She covered her mouth and, kneeling down, gasped, 'Oh, oh, no, no...'

Warton locked the door, shoved his gun back into its holster, and strode over to where Laia knelt. He grabbed her by the hair and dragged her howling over to the sofa. Throwing her upon it, he began to yank her slacks off.

***

Following Q'zar's orders, Chu went to Laia's apartment first. He was puzzled at seeing no guard at the door. Hearing screams from inside, he tried the door. Finding it was locked, he drew his gun before inserting the master key.

Warton froze when he saw Chu enter. He stood up, pulled his trousers up and began buckling his belt. They stared at one another.

Laia crawled away from him.

With his gun trained on Warton, Chu flipped his telecom open.

'This is your last time, Warton.'

'What're you saying? The bitch wanted it. Anyway, what are you doing out? Good to see you, man,' Warton bantered, realizing that Chu had not noticed Arron's body which was partly hid by the sofa.

'Take your shooter out and throw it over there,' Chu said. 'Slowly.' Warton did so. He watched his gun spin across the carpet.

'I don't think you're glad to see me out,' said Chu. 'I think you put me in there. It's urgent, put me through now,' Chu shouted into his telecom. It was then that he noticed Arron's feet.

Shakily, Laia got up to her feet and tottered over where Chu stood in front of the door.

Not taking his eyes off Warton for a second, Chu reached for a coat that hung behind Laia and handed it her. She pulled it on.

Getting no response from Security, Chu began to think what he should do.

Warton nodded toward the window and said, 'Sounds like a war going on out there.'

'Don't try anything, Warton,' Chu snapped, his eyes glued to Warton's every move.

When Warton turned, he smiled.

Chu gave a gasp of pain.

Laia swung round. She saw a knife come out of Chu's back as he staggered forward. Warton rushed at him. Chu fired. Warton clutched his stomach. A second shot made his face twist in agony as his knees gave beneath him. Both sank to the floor almost banging their heads as they fell.

Laia's gaze was riveted upon the black-gloved hand that held the blood-smeared knife. She knew that hand. But the face that stepped into view startled her. It wore the mask of another age. The masked figure slammed the door shut and raised the knife like a mantis ready to strike.

Laia stumbled back, as the howling mouth of the Noh mask followed her. When she felt her head bang up against a cupboard she knew she could retreat no further. She was trapped at the end of the short passage between the breakfast bar and electric cooker. She readied herself to grab the arm that held the knife. One, no; two, no; three, no, not yet, not yet...

The room shook violently.

Laia grabbed the edges to the worktops on either side to stop from falling. In the same instant, she saw Zuriko thrown to the floor. She rushed forward, slamming drawers that had slid open barring her way as she did so. As she turned toward the door, she saw Zuriko on all fours scrambling to pick up the knife that she had dropped. The room was still swaying and china crashing onto the floor as Laia rushed into the corridor.

She was bouncing off the sides of the corridor as she raced toward the Midround. Reaching it, she tore into an open elevator and gasped, 'Ground level'.

She was about to sink down onto the floor when she realized the elevator had not responded. She sprang forward and slammed her hand on the 'shut doors' button. As the doors closed, the elevator flashed an 'out of service' sign. Frantically, she held the button down.

***

The destruction of one of the oldest bio-dome pillars had sent shockwaves throughout the Tower. When the Tower's shaking died down and became a slow sway, a secretary turned and said, 'It's the enemy. Asking for the Chairman.' He held a telecom out for Darvin to take.

Darvin was trembling, rubbing his mouth. He stared at the telecom.

'Take it! For Code's sake, will someone take it!' screamed Sovran, snatching the telecom from the secretary's hand and sticking it into Darvin's.

Darvin stuttered, 'I am Darvin, Chairman of...' He gulped, as the machine voice of a robot interrupted with a demand for immediate and unconditional surrender. Darvin turned to the others, 'If we don't surrender, it says they'll destroy the Tower.' No one spoke. The hopelessness of their position was obvious. Q'zar's head dropped. Darvin choked, 'We surrender.'

A secretary pointed to the screen he had linked to the call. All eyes turned to it. There, they saw Sapor.

'All forces at Ground Level to disarm and leave the Tower. All directors and nobles to remain at Topround. All civil servants to proceed to Midround and wait for our arrival in the auditorium. It is there that you will sign the terms of the surrender in one hour's time as dictated by our revered leader Moran II, descendant of Koron III. Any further resistance will result in the destruction of the Tower.'

***

When the Tower steadied, the elevator responded. Reaching ground floor, Laia stepped out into mayhem. She pressed herself against a wall to get out of the way of the stampede. Someone screamed at her to run. When she didn't, another grabbed her by the arm and pulled her headlong onto a walkway. She clung to one side as people rushed past. They were all running, running, running.

Oblivious to the announcements of surrender blaring overhead and instructions to citizen and clone alike to return to their homes and stay indoors, warning against resistance, and reassuring everyone that the situation was under control, she was carried further and further from the Tower.

When the walkway finally came to an end, she tripped off. Without looking where she was going, she stumbled down to street level. It was pitch dark. Looking around, she could not recognize the district. People were swarming around like shadows. Some were crying, others lay groaning on the ground and many were being carried. Swept into the throng, she noticed crowds trying to pull the injured out from under fallen masonry. All around, people were crying for help. She coughed as the dust caught in her throat. Not looking where she was going, she bumped into someone. A stocky woman. They looked into the shadows of one another's faces mumbling apologies. They made to pass one another again but blocked each other's way by stepping in the same direction.

'Are you okay?' the woman asked, seeing how beaten and blood-stained Laia's face was.

'....'

When Laia's coat fell open and the woman saw that she wore nothing, she said, 'Here, let me help you.'

She led Laia by the hand. One look into Laia's eyes told her everything she needed to know.

'Come on,' she said, putting an arm around her and guiding her through a complicated pattern of lanes to a ramshackle shed.

Once inside, she made Laia sit down and set about making her a hot drink. After she had taken some sips, she dabbed the blood off her face. As Laia felt her ordeal shift to the really happened and really was, she was wracked with heart-rending sobs.

Eva hugged her as a sister.

The Joypolis Series

Clone City is 1 of 7 in *The Joypolis Series*. The next in the series is entitled *The New Order*. Here's an extract:

From *Joypolis 2: The New Order*

'Eva you've got to rest. If you don't, you'll get ill,' Laia said, seeing sadness drain the life out of her face. Codes, she thought, how many times do I have to tell her before she listens? She looked as if she was on the brink of a nervous breakdown.

Staring out over the tops of some huts that were lower down, Eva replied, 'It's us they want. Don't you see? If you stay, they'll take you, too. I'm sorry, Laia, but you've got to go.'

Laia knew she had overstayed. She had a lot to thank Eva for. She had given her refuge and enough love and care for her to regain enough confidence to step outside. But what had started with gentle hints like, 'Where are you going when you get better?' and 'Isn't it time you thought about going back?' or 'Your friends will be worried, won't they?' had become blunter until she was telling her to go. She decided she had better leave. That was about a week ago. But she came back when she found that no one was allowed in or out of the Tower. Eva was none too pleased to see her come back. She had her own problems. The hard work she was being forced to do must have something to do with it, Laia thought. Her moods now swung from fair to furious. Laia supposed she wanted to be left alone to face whatever the future held. She just wished there was something, anything, she could do to help. But this time, she knew she would have to go for good. She could not keep putting it off.

With a sad smile, she said, 'I'll leave this afternoon. About five. Okay?'

Eva patted her hand and asked, 'Where'll you go?'

'The Maze. It's got a reputation as a place where you can get anything you want at a price.' Looking up at Eva whose crate was slightly higher than hers, Laia smiled. 'Don't worry, I'll be all right.' She knew she could not face going back to her apartment. Not yet. Not after what had happened there. She'd go tell the Watchers first. If she could find any.

Joypolis 2, *The New Order*, will soon be available. For more information, as well as advance ordering, please visit
www.adrianpetersauthor.com
For questions or comments, please use the email contact form on the website.